UNIKKAAQT

An Introduction to Inuit Myths and Legends

UNIKKAAQTUAT

An Introduction to Inuit Myths and Legends

Edited by
Neil Christopher
Noel McDermott
Louise Flaherty

Researched, Compiled, and Annotated by
Neil Christopher

Introduction and Chapter Notes by
Noel McDermott

Published by Inhabit Media Inc.
www.inhabitmedia.com

Toronto Office -146A Orchard View Blvd., Toronto, Ontario, M4R 1C3
Iqaluit Office - P.O. Box 11125, Iqaluit, Nunavut, X0A 1H0

This book is the result of a coordinated initiative between the Nunavut Bilingual Education Society, Nunavut Arcitc College, the Nunavut Teacher Education Program, the Qikiqtani Inuit Association., Canadian Heritage and the Department of Culture, Language, Elders and Youth (Government of Nunavut).

Printed and bound in Canada

0 1 2 3 4 5 6 7 8 9

ISBN 978-1-926569-16-1

Library and Archives Canada Cataloguing in Publication

Unikkaaqtuat : an introduction to Inuit myths and legends / researched and gathered by Neil Christopher ; introduction by Noel McDermott.

ISBN 978-1-926569-16-1

1. Inuit--Canada--Folklore. 2. Inuit mythology. 3. Legends--Arctic regions. I. Christopher, Neil, 1972-

E99.E7U543 2011 398.2089'9712 C2010-908108-0

ᓄᓇᕗᑦ ᓯᓚᑦᑐᖅᓴᕐᕕᒃ
Nunavut
Arctic College

ᕿᑭᖅᑕᓂ ᐃᓄᐃᑦ ᑲᑐᔨᖃᑎᒌᖏᑦ
Qikiqtani Inuit Association

ᓄᓇᕗᑦ
Nunavut

Canadian   Patrimoine
Heritage   canadien

Table of Contents

Chapter Six

Animal Fables **259**

Editors' Note

This collection of stories has been created with the oldest versions of each story that I found in my research.

The text has been edited where sense and grammar dictated, however, the original spellings of people and places have been retained.

For those familiar with the Arctic and Inuit place names, you may notice that in several stories the identified region where the story was recorded and the place names within the story do not match. Inuit were great travellers. So, a story recorded in one region may have been heard somewhere else.

Introduction

*U*nikkaaqtuat: An Introduction to Traditional Inuit Myths and Legends will be of interest both to readers new to the subject of traditional Inuit stories and also to those who have already made acquaintance with this unique and fascinating genre. Many of the stories here were first recorded by Rasmussen, Boas, Jenness, and Rink, whose names will be familiar to those readers who have knowledge of Inuit history and culture. Readers who wish to explore Inuit myths and traditional stories further would do well to consult the work of these early pioneers in the field of Inuit anthropology. The editor and compiler of these myths, Neil Christopher, has endeavoured to seek out the first recorded accounts of the stories included in this volume in order to get as close as possible to the original telling and to avoid the accretions and additions which necessarily accumulate as stories are retold and retranslated by different individuals over time. Versions of the same story appear side by side in this volume, which allows the reader to compare them and to see how the basic story is recounted in another region.

The stories in this volume are divided into six chapters and each section is prefaced with a short introduction giving an indication of some of the themes and characteristics the reader will encounter. The text is also punctuated with comments in the margin that are aimed to explain words, ideas, or actions with which a reader unfamiliar with the topic might have difficulty. However, it is important to remember that such notes are not intended to be exhaustive or prescriptive, but are offered as a guide and no more. The attentive reader will soon be able to see for herself connections and meanings that have been overlooked in the notes. A number of characteristics and themes may be identified running through the legends here. The story of Atanaarjuat, which appears in this volume, is used to briefly identify some of them. This is then followed with a more detailed account of some of the other major themes.

The reader will likely be familiar with the story of Atanaarjuat because of the success of the movie version directed by Zacharias Kunuk of Isuma Productions from Igloolik, Nunavut. The film won the Caméra d'Or prize at the Cannes Film Festival in 2001 and was acclaimed by many as a masterpiece. The movie stays very close to the original story and provides an excellent entry into the world of traditional Inuit culture. The action is initiated by jealousy on the part of hunters who are less successful than Atanaarjuat and his brother Aamarjuaq. Envy is a common theme in these stories and often leads to disaster, as is the case for Atanaarjuat. The other hunters plot to kill Atanaarjuat and while they succeed in eliminating his brother, Atanaarjuat escapes, having been warned by an old woman. Relentlessly pursued by his enemies, Atanaarjuat outruns them and is given shelter and a place to hide by an old couple. Old people, women in particular, are often the mediators or means of preservation in traditional stories. They heal Atanaarjuat's wounds and he plans his revenge, which is typically calculated and detailed as it is in other stories. No one escapes the anger of Atanaarjuat, and he mercilessly clubs everyone to death. Violence in these legends is never softened and is often graphic and horrible. Atanaarjuat takes control of the camp, allows the wives of the killed hunters to live, and has their sons do the hunting and other necessary work. The story ends by noting that nothing is known about Atanaarjuat's later life or how he died. In this story, as in many others, nothing is resolved. Widows and orphans must depend on and take orders from the killer of their husbands, brothers, and fathers. What appears to be a resolution has all the potential to become a living nightmare. Envy, violence, murder, revenge, and a problematic ending are some of the main themes and characteristics of this and other stories. The magic in the film is not included in the version of the story in this volume.

Magic is, however, an essential component of traditional Inuit myths, and without it the actions in many of the stories simply could not happen. The term magic as used here should not be confused with the modern concept of trickery or sleight of hand. Rather, it is intended to mean, in the broadest possible way, any action that cannot be explained by reason alone. These stories are full of such actions. Related to the theme of magic is the person of the angakkuq or shaman, who could be either male or female, and who possessed powers not available to ordinary people. An angakkuq could be identified by special markings on articles of clothing and by the presence of many amulets or charms, such as a bone, a rabbit foot, or another piece of animal skin. Respected and feared by the community, the angakkuq could see into the future, cure the sick, direct hunters to where animals could be found, expose those who broke taboos, kill his or her enemies, and, most importantly, visit the sea goddess Sedna to ask that she release the animals from captivity to relieve the suffering of starving people. The angakkuq could not depend on his or her powers alone. After serving an apprenticeship with another angakkuq, tuurngait (helping spirits) were called upon to assist in the work. The tuurngaq could be anything, an animal or object, but the more powerful animals were the more useful helpers, and the polar bear is one that appears consistently throughout these stories.

Transformation is a theme common in these stories as it is in the stories of other cultures. Animals often change to human shape and humans change into animal shape. This kind of change implies a lot more than simple disguise, though that is clearly an important element. The stories in Chapter One, "How the World Came to Be and Other Creation Stories," tell of a time when humans and animals lived together as one. Even though they maintained their individual shapes and retained their unique characteristics, they shared language and dwellings and hunted in the same manner. Bears ate as bears normally do, foxes maintained their distinctive smell, and humans walked upright, but this was an inclusive world inhabited by men and beasts on equal terms. This is a very different world than that in which the princess kisses the frog only to discover it is, in reality, a prince. In Inuit traditional stories the animals are not humans waiting to be released from their prison state, but complete and autonomous inhabitants of the world where they interact with, and exchange form with, their human counterparts.

Another theme prominent in the myths included here is fear of strangers. Frequently, as travellers approach a village new to them, they move cautiously and with suspicion. This is understandable when we consider the huge expanses of land and sea where Inuit travelled and lived without contact with other people besides their own relatives and group. Strangers or visitors were few, and it was prudent to exercise caution when encountering them. This fear, therefore, has a pragmatic basis which makes it a sensible and useful social tool, but it may also be related to the idea of transformation. One could never be sure that the person who approached was indeed human. It might actually be a bear, ready to wreak havoc on the village and its inhabitants. Caution could literally save one's life.

An important purpose of all Inuit stories is to teach a lesson or lessons; however, the moral to be learned is not always overt or plainly stated. Rather, the Inuit way of teaching is by inference so that those for whom the story is intended are neither singled out nor referred to. The reader is, therefore, encouraged to ask the question, "What is the teaching here?" There is no right or wrong answer to this question—how could we possibly know?—but there are answers that, if they are consistent with and evolve from the details of the story, will satisfy. There is a body of stories, however, where the lessons to be learned are transparent, and examples of this can be read in Chapter Six, "Animal Fables." Readers acquainted with Aesop's Fables will be familiar with the type and will recognize a similar pattern here. Often vanity, naivety, or inexperience, or a combination of these, leads one character to humiliation, a loss of possessions, or even death. What is characteristic of these stories is their lack of sentimentality and the sheer self-interest out of which the protagonists behave.

Another dominant characteristic found in these myths is violence, which invariably leads to murder. There is hardly one story in this collection that does not feature violence in some form, physical or emotional, and the violence is often premeditated and cruel in the extreme. A common catalyst for violent action is anger and jealousy, whether related to a wife's infidelity, real or imagined, or a hunter's envy of the skills and achievements of another. A single violent action often leads to even more killing in retaliation and what ensues is a blood feud so that the outcome is unsatisfactory and only leads to further violence. Revenge is, therefore, a common theme. One family member often urges a survivor to plan and execute the death of those responsible for murdering a father, brother, or other relative. Many stories have no clear resolution, and the future is left uncertain and unpredictable. This may be expected of a society which lived so close to the elements of nature in its most extreme form. Predicting what may happen tomorrow must have seemed like an outrageous and insupportable impertinence.

Students of traditional Inuit stories can readily distinguish those stories which adhere closely to original practices from those which are of a later vintage. Stories retold and reinterpreted frequently provide explanations for the actions in the stories. The oldest versions of the myths, which include many of the stories in this volume, are characterized by a lack of explanation within the story itself. The reader is left to accept, or to attempt to interpret, just why characters are motivated to behave in the way they do. This can be disconcerting to the modern reader, who expects characters to behave in a manner consistent with what one may describe as normal human practices. This, of course, raises the question: what is normal human practice? Lacking a satisfactory answer, readers may be best advised to suspend their disbelief and to enter into the spirit of the story. In this way, previous and preconceived notions of normalcy may be temporarily laid aside and the norms and nuances of the legend allowed to speak for themselves.

The orphan is a recurrent figure in Inuit traditional stories, and the hardness of traditional life ensured that orphans were not in short supply. Orphans in these stories usually live with their grandmothers on the margins of society, and are subjected to the most intense cruelty and humiliation by all the villagers. They are given the most menial of tasks to perform, such as emptying the chamber pots and rendering seal fat for the qulliq, the stone lamp. They are obliged to sleep in the porch of the snow house with the dogs and feed on scraps. A few people in the village, usually women, treat orphans with compassion. Eventually the orphan grows in strength and exacts a fearsome revenge on the tormentors, taking a place in society as head of a new family. The orphan usually grows up to become a difficult and dangerous person. The moral may seem to be clear: don't mistreat orphans or they will get their revenge. However, the stories raise other disturbing questions about the kind of society that contains such a person. The orphan is not portrayed as the likeable conquering hero, but rather is vengeful, calculating, and extremely cruel to those he allows to live. It is the values of the whole society that are called into question and not the actions of one or two persons.

Another common feature of these stories is how often old people, usually women, are abandoned or forced to live apart from the main camp. Frequently these old women have a grandchild living with them—sometimes, but not invariably, a girl. In traditional Inuit society each person was required to make a contribution to the camp. The vagaries of the hunt and the weather meant that food and clothing were often at a premium and the prospect of starvation very real. Therefore, those who contributed least or who were a burden on the resources of the camp were the most expendable. Too many girls were a cause for concern, as were the old or infirm, and so they were the ones most likely to be left behind when the people of the camp moved on. This was not done out of malice or spite but in order to give the best chance of survival to those who were healthiest and likely to live. Of course, as many of the stories here attest, those who unnecessarily abandoned or abused older people might live to regret their actions.

Problems in marriage can often lead to tragedy in these stories. It is important to remember that marriages were arranged in traditional Inuit society. The idea of romantic love, which dominates the relationships between couples in western society, had no relevance for Inuit. The western insistence on individual responsibility and choice was completely at odds with Inuit ideas of community. Couples married because it was the thing to do. They were told to do so by their elders, who had already arranged and chosen partners for them, often while the couple were still infants. What mattered most was the community and the continuance of society, not what an individual wished. A girl who refused to marry was, therefore, not simply exercising her own will but deliberately and emphatically defying and rejecting the norms of Inuit society. Her behaviour threated the very existence of the group, which depended on its members to follow the traditions in order to ensure its survival. There were, and still are in some regions, strict guidelines governing the behaviours of males and females. For example, a father-in-law was not allowed to address his daughter-in-law directly and vice versa. Such fastidiousness did not extend to the behaviour of the married couple, who could engage in wife swapping if they desired. The consequences were not always happy, and jealousy and anger often gives way to wife abuse and breakup of the marriage. Wives who cheat on their husbands are treated with disdain and punished severely.

Marriage, however, was not a luxury but a necessity. In many of the stories we read about hunters who, on arrival at a camp, find a woman living alone and immediately take her as a wife. Hunters will even take an animal for a wife—a fox, a goose, or a raven being most common. This of course sounds strange to the modern reader, and it is. But, for traditional Inuit men and women, the importance of having a partner cannot be overstated. It was simply too difficult to survive without one. The man provided the food, skins, and shelter, and also made the tools needed both for hunting and use in the camp. The woman prepared the meat, cleaned the skins, made and repaired the clothing, and bore and cared for the children. Their mutual interdependence ensured that each one had a role and a responsibility to the other. While a man could prepare and sew clothing, and a woman could hunt, working together gave them a better chance of survival. Not the least of the attractions was the fact that companionship, especially where man and wife were compatible, made a normally demanding and difficult lifestyle more palatable.

In a world peopled with spirits, Inuit were exhorted to be careful about how they used words. One never knew who or what might overhear a conversation and use it to their advantage against the speaker. Words were to be used sparingly, and idle chatter was frowned upon and discouraged. Inuit believed in the power of words to create whatever was spoken. Thus, night and day were made because both the fox and the hare wished it to be so, each to suit its own needs. Parents taught their children to be careful what they wished for, even if they were not serious, because they might regret the consequences. This is precisely what happens in the "Story of Three Girls." The girls speak aloud about their preferences for a husband. While two of the girls are rescued from their unwanted marriages, the third is condemned to suffer a living death as she gradually turns to stone; a severe consequence for a piece of childish fancy.

Many of the myths in this book are peopled with monsters and strange creatures which are the stuff of nightmares. It is difficult, if not impossible, for any person living in Canada today, Inuit or non-Inuit, to imagine what it was like to live as Inuit traditionally did. The sheer vastness of the land, the extremes of climate, the long winter nights and the lack of contact with other peoples created a fertile imaginative space in which the unfamiliar became frightening, threatening, and real. Gathered around the dim light of the qulliq, the stories being told assumed a power of their own and became part of everyday life and experience. The people with long fingernails, those with no anuses, spider women, dwarfs, giants, cannibals, shadow people, child-stealers, and the rest were a formidable crew, which one discounted at one's peril. The air was literally filled with such monsters and Inuit had to be on their guard lest they fall prey to their machinations. Not all strange creatures were malignant, but vigilance was a necessary tool to ensure one was not caught unawares.

Taboos helped Inuit to live in right relationship with their environment, especially the animals on which they depended for survival. A breach of taboo could potentially threaten not only the individual guilty person but the whole camp. Traditional Inuit society was highly regulated and order was maintained by observing many different taboos. There were rules governing every single aspect of life: childbirth, naming, death, eating, sewing, hunting, and so on. As one might expect, a large number of taboos revolved around the proper care and treatment of animals without which Inuit could not survive. It was believed that animals gave themselves to the hunters, and so it was incumbent on the Inuit to show respect for this favour. Failure to do so could result in a scarcity of animals, as the soul of the offended one would inform others who would refuse to be caught. As a sign of respect and acknowledgement of this belief, the hunter had to perform certain actions to propitiate the soul of the animal. For example, a hunter would cover the eyes of a fish with soot to ensure the fisherman would not be recognized. A seal was given a drink of fresh water so that it would not report negatively on the person who had killed it.

Out of necessity, Inuit used every part of an animal they caught. This also ensured there was no wastage of precious food. Sharing of food was another sign of respect, and also insurance against future need when the action would be reciprocated. A hunter should never boast about his catch because the spirits of the animals might be listening and could take offence. Pregnant women were not allowed to eat certain foods nor eat from the same pot as their husbands; some women could eat meat given to them by particular men but not from others; clothing had to be sewn a certain way; women were not allowed to be out too long at night; only men were allowed to eat a first catch, and so on. Inuit feared, above all, angering the spirit Sedna, who was said to control all the sea mammals, and so they went out of their way not to transgress any of the taboos associated with her. Taboos varied from group to group but they all had the same purpose: to ensure good weather and hunting by avoiding offending the spirits that controlled and inhabited the same world as Inuit.

Chapter Three, "Journeys and Adventures," includes stories about Kiviuq, an important character of epic proportion whose stories are found across the circumpolar world. Like the hero of Greek myth, Odysseus, Kiviuq wanders far and wide trying to get back home. Having survived a storm which drowns all the other hunters, Kiviuq has to rely on his own resources to stay alive. However, he is not entirely alone. He has two spirit helpers to aid him: a bird and a bear. On his way, he encounters many obstacles and sees many strange things. His life is threatened and he is many times in imminent danger, but with a combination of good fortune and a little help from his spirit friends, Kiviuq overcomes all difficulties and finally returns home.

Kiviuq's homecoming is not the unmitigated joyful occasion one might anticipate. Time has passed, people have changed, and difficult and painful adjustments have to be made to accommodate the returned Kiviuq. Each of the many episodes in Kiviuq's travels has something to teach and the lessons are often hard-won. But, overall, there are two aspects of the Kiviuq legend which stand out. One is that even the most resourceful of persons at some time or another needs help, no matter how independent or powerful one may be. The other thing worthy of note is that Kiviuq never gives up. Every setback, and there are many, is a temporary delay as he relentlessly continues his journey.

These two points may help to answer the question of how relevant these stories are today. While they are entertaining and give the reader a glimpse into the traditional world of Inuit, they also provide useful lessons on how we might live in a world which appears to be growing more chaotic, unpredictable, and dangerous.

In many of the stories, the narrator names the particular place where the events take place. This gives a sense of reality and credibility to the incidents. It is as if the teller is saying, "What I am telling you really did happen and I can show you just where." But no matter how localized the action may be, two aspects remain unknown: we never know when the story was first told or who told it. This has the opposite effect to that produced by naming the place of origin. There is a sense of timelessness about these myths which suggests that they are deeply rooted in the culture and traditions of the people. They are simply part of who and what Inuit are and need no further authentication. This sense of timelessness is further reinforced by the universality of the themes that are addressed in the stories. Envy, anger, violence, anti-social behaviour, and the struggle to make meaningful community are not confined to the pages of this volume, but are the common inheritance of all humankind. The original storytellers did not waste time trying to describe the ideal life. They did even better. They allowed individual listeners to reflect on their part in seeking to maintain order and community by showing clearly and without hesitation the destructive forces of self-interest at work.

The general impression a reader may take away from the stories in this collection may be one of a world full of cruelty, murder, and chaos, leaving many questions unanswered and discrepancies unresolved. This is inevitable when the stories, as we have them, lack the explanation or exegesis of knowledgeable contemporary Inuit. However, if the reader accepts the premise that these stories had two main purposes, to entertain and to teach, then it is possible to begin to understand that there is a consistently implied message throughout. Behind all the described chaos, violence, and gratuitous cruelty the stories point to what the norm is and ought to be. If a hunter kills his companion because he is jealous of his accomplishments and is in turn plotted against, pursued, and murdered by relatives of the dead man, then clearly there is no satisfactory resolution. The relatives of both parties are condemned to repeat the mistakes of their forebears. The lesson to be learned is clear: jealousy is the most destructive of emotions and should be avoided at all cost. This is especially true in small, close-knit communities such as Inuit lived in, where everyone knows everyone else. The girl who refuses to marry is not making a courageous and laudable individual stand against the tyranny of her parents. She is denying all that makes her society work—respect for elders and the traditions they embody. The world of violence and chaos is the opposite of what a functioning and enduring society should be, and this is essentially what these stories have to teach.

Noel McDermott

How the World Came to Be and Other Creation Stories

This chapter is, as the title implies, about how certain things came to be. This is an age-old question and one answered by Inuit in their own way.

The reader may want to be on the lookout for the following:

- *Animals and humans living side by side*
- *Magic words that have a creative power*
- *The introduction of death*
- *Children who are not born, but obtained*
- *Thunder and lightning as young thieves*
- *The woman who refuses to marry and becomes a mighty spirit*
- *Transformation and magic*
- *The mistreatment of step-children*
- *Shape-shifting as a regular occurrence*
- *The angakkuq*

The Struggle for Day and Night

This version is from the Netsilik region.

This story introduces the reader to the concept that in ancient times animals were like people and had the power of speech and the ability to assume human form. The story also illustrates the power and magic of the spoken word.

In the very first times there was no light on earth. Everything was in darkness: the lands could not be seen, the animals could not be seen. Both people and animals lived on the earth, but there was no difference between them. They lived indiscriminately: a person could become an animal and an animal could become a human being. There were wolves, bears, and foxes, but as soon as they turned into humans they were all the same. They may have had different habits, but all spoke the same language, lived in the same kind of house, and spoke and hunted in the same way.

That is the way they lived here on earth in the very earliest times, times that no one can understand now. That was the time when magic words were made. A word spoken by chance would suddenly become powerful, and what people wanted to happen could happen, and nobody could explain how it came to be.

In those times when everyone lived together and there was no difference between humans and animals, a fox and a hare met.

"Taaq-taaq-taaq: Darkness-darkness-darkness," said the fox. It liked the dark when it was going out to steal from the caches of the humans.

"Ublu-ublu-ublu: Day-day-day," said the hare. It wanted the light of day, so that it could find a place to feed.

Suddenly the sky became as the hare wished it to be; its words were the most powerful. Day came and replaced night, and when night had gone day came again. Light and dark took turns with each other.

Origin of Death

This version is from the South Baffin region.

There were a great many Inuit on Milliqjuaq. There were also a great many people on all the other islands of the Earth. At that time there had never been a death. There were a few islands, which were floating about. The islands did not touch the bottom of the sea. The people on Milliqjuaq came to be so numerous that the island became top-heavy and turned over. Thus a great many people were killed. These were the first deaths. Ever since that time, humans have continued to die. A long time after this event the waters began to recede, and the islands went aground. At the time when the waters receded, a whale was left ashore, and walruses were left at Lake Netchilik.

According to the following story, in the earliest times the sea level was much higher than it is now. The entire population lived on a few floating islands.

The reference to walrus and whales is intended to explain why marine mammal bones have been found out on the land well away from the sea.

How Children were Formerly Obtained

This version is from the Kivalliq region.

It is often told that in the beginning the land itself bore children. Some versions explain that male children were more difficult to find than female children.

I n olden times the women did not bear children, but when they wanted one, they went out and searched on the ground until they found one. Some women were unable to find children.

Thunder and Lightning

This version is from the Netsilik region.

The thunder and the lightning were children of the same parents, two poor orphans, who had no relatives at all. They once lived on Netsilik land, but when the people crossed a river in search of caribou, these two were left behind to die of hunger. No one felt kindness towards them. They were only a burden.

Then why did they go up to the sky? Well, it has been said that evil actions populate the sky, but that does not mean that those who go up into the sky are the evil ones. It may be that others make life impossible and intolerable for those who should live on earth. Revenge often comes in a strange and inconceivable manner.

The two poor orphans who were to die of hunger went to a garbage heap to see if they could find something that had been forgotten by the people who had abandoned them. One of them found a firestone and the other a stump of caribou skin, and with these things in their hands they cried to each other:

The mistreatment of orphans is a very common theme in traditional Inuit stories. Often a supernatural force intervenes and provides the mistreated children with the power they need to punish those who have done them harm. This is the case in this version of the origin of thunder and lightning.

The storyteller prefaced this tale with, "But sun and moon and stars, thunder and lightning, are all people who once have gone out into space. Why? Well, that cannot be explained. We never ask about that ourselves. And still, it has a reason. Evil actions and taboo-breakings have populated the air with spirits. The sun and the moon murdered their mother, and, though they were brother and sister, they loved each other. For that reason they ceased to be humans."

"What shall we be?"

"Thunder and lightning!"

At that time neither of them knew what thunder and lightning were; but suddenly they rose into the sky and one struck sparks with the firestone, while the other drummed on the dried caribou skin until the heavens roared. For the first time it thundered and lightning shot over the earth. The two hovered over the village where the people were that had wanted them to starve to death. They killed them, people and dogs, simply by rushing across the sky over their tents. Those who found them later wondered how they had died, for they were not changed at all and had no wounds; only their eyes were bloodshot with terror. But when people touched them they fell into ashes.

The Brother and Sister who Became Thunder and Lightning

This version is from the Kivalliq region.

Here is another version of how thunder and lightning came to exist. In this version the theme of mistreatment and consequence is not so prominent.

In the earliest times, there was no such thing as stealing. There were no thieves among mankind. But then one day, during a song festival, a brother and sister were left alone in a house. They found a caribou skin with the hair removed and a flint rock. These they stole, but hardly had they stolen them when a great fear of being caught by others in their village came upon them.

"What shall we do to get away from everyone?" said one.

"Let us turn into caribou," said the other.

"Then people will kill us."

"Let us turn into wolves."

"Then people will kill us."

"Let us turn into foxes."

And so they went through all animals in turn and always they were afraid people would kill them. But then one said: "Let us turn into thunder and lightning, and then people will not be able to catch us."

So they turned into thunder and lightning and went up into the sky. When there is thunder and lightning now, it is because one of them rattles the dry caribou skin, while the other strikes the flint rock and sends sparks across the sky.

Origin of the Sun and the Moon

This version is from the South Baffin region.

The story of how the sun and moon came to exist varies slightly from region to region. Most versions involve a brother and sister, and the breaking of a taboo: incest.

In a village a woman lived in a hut all by herself. One evening, while the people were assembled in their dancing house, a man went to the woman, put out her lamps, and compelled her to sleep with him. After this he came to the woman's hut every night while the people were in the dancing house. The woman wanted to know who he was. She asked him often, but he did not tell his name or utter a sound. Since she was unable to convince him to tell her his name, she resorted to a ruse. One day, after he arrived, she rubbed her fingers across the bottom of one of her pots, and then across the left side of his face. After a while he left her. She followed him to the dancing house and heard much laughter coming from inside. She went in, and there she saw that the people were laughing at her own brother, who bore the marks of her fingers on the left side of his face. After seeing that she took a knife, cut off her left breast, and offered it to him, saying, "Eat this." She took up a piece of wood, such as is used for trimming lamps, and lit it. He also took a trimming-stick in his left hand, lit it, and followed her. She went out of the dancing house and ran around it, pursued by her brother. Finally her brother fell. The flame on his stick went out, while hers continued to burn brightly. They were wafted up to the sky. She became the sun, and he became the moon.

The Mother of the Sea Mammals

This version was recorded in the South Baffin region. Although, the name Uinigumissuitung (which translates as "the woman who doesn't want to take a husband") is found in North Baffin versions.

I n Padli lived a girl named Avilayoq. Since she did not want to have a husband, she was also called Uinigumissuitung.

There was a red and white speckled stone in the camp where Avilayoq lived. The stone transformed itself into a dog and married Avilayoq. She had many dog-children, some of whom were the ancestors of Inuit, others white men, others Inuarudligat, Ijiqat, and Adlet. The children made a great deal of noise, which annoyed Avilayoq's father so much that he finally took them across to the island Amituaqdjuausiq. Every day Avilayoq sent her husband across the channel to her father's hut to get meat for herself and her children. She fastened a pair of boots around her husband's neck with a string. Every day her father filled the boots with meat, and the dog took them back to the island.

One day, while the dog was gone for meat, a man came to the island in his kayak and called Uinigumissuitung.

"Take your bag and come with me!" he shouted.

He had the appearance of a tall, good-looking man and Avilayoq

This story is perhaps the most widely know Inuit traditional story. In it, the origin of Inuit, other races, and many sea animals are explained. As well, this story introduces the mother of the sea mammals. She is known by many names in many different regions, but she is feared in all of them. In the past, she was the one who insured that all taboos were respected.

Inuarudligat and Ijiqat are supernatural beings, and Adlet is the Inuit term for First Nations peoples.

According to another version, he wore snow-goggles made of walrus-ivory, and he said, "Do you see my snow-goggles?" and then laughed at her because she began to cry.

found him attractive. She took her bag, went down to the kayak, and the suitor paddled away with her. After they had gone some distance, they came to a cake of floating ice. The man stepped out of the kayak onto the ice and Avilayoq noticed that he was quite a small man, and that he appeared large only because he had been sitting on a high seat.

She began to cry because she had been deceived. He simply laughed and said, "Oh, you have seen my seat, have you?"

Then he went back into his kayak and they proceeded on their journey. Finally, they came to a place where there were many people and many huts. The stranger landed the kayak. He pointed out to her a certain hut made of the skins of yearling seals, told her that it was his, and said that she was to go there. The woman went up to the hut, while he attended to his kayak. He soon joined her in the hut and stayed with her for three or four days before going out again sealing. Her new husband was a petrel.

Meanwhile, her father had left the dog, her former husband, at his house, and went to look for her on the island. When he did not find her, he returned home and told the dog to wait there for him, as he was going in search of his daughter. He set out in a large boat, travelled for a long time, and visited many places but did not find her. Finally, he came to the place where she lived. He saw many huts and, without leaving his boat, he shouted and called to his daughter to return home with him. She came down from her hut and boarded her father's boat, where he hid her among some skins.

They had not been gone long when they noticed a man in a kayak following them. It was her new husband, the petrel. He soon overtook them. When he came alongside their boat, he asked the young woman to show her hand. He was very anxious to see at least part of her body to confirm it was his wife, but she did not move. Then he asked her to show her mitten, but again she did not respond to his request. He tried many times to convince her to show parts of her body to prove her identity, but she refused. Then he began to cry, resting his head on his arms, which were crossed in front of the manhole of the kayak. Avilayoq's father paddled on as fast as he could, and the man fell far behind.

The water was calm and they continued on their way home. After a while, they saw something coming from behind toward their boat, but they could not see it clearly. Sometimes it looked like a man in a kayak. Sometimes it looked like a petrel. It flew up and down, then skimmed over the water, and finally it came up to their boat and flew round and round their kayak several times before it disappeared again. Suddenly ripples appeared, the waters began to rise and, after a short time, a gale began to rage. The boat was quite a distance from shore. The old man became afraid that they might drown. Fearing the revenge of his daughter's husband, he threw her into the water. The daughter refused to be left behind in the sea and held on to the gunwale. The father took his hatchet and chopped off the first joints of her fingers. When they fell into the water, they were transformed into whales, the nails becoming the whalebone and baleen.

Still, she clung to the boat. Again he took his hatchet and chopped off the second joints of her fingers. They were transformed into ground seals. Still, she clung to the boat. Then he chopped off the last joints of her fingers, which were transformed into seals. She clung to the boat now with only the stumps of her hands. Her father took his steering oar and knocked out her left eye. She finally fell backward into the water and he paddled away, leaving his daughter to the waves. Eventually, he returned to his camp.

Back at his camp, he filled with stones the boots used by the dog to carry meat to his family. He covered the top of the stones with meat to make the dog think he was carrying his usual load. The dog started to swim across the channel, but when he was halfway across, the heavy stones dragged him down. He began to sink and was drowned. A great noise was heard while he was drowning. The father took down his tent and went down to the beach at the time of low water. There, he lay down and covered himself with the tent. Eventually, the tide rose over him and when the waters receded he had disappeared.

Avilayoq became Sedna, who lives in the lower world, in her house built of stone and whale ribs. She has but one eye and she cannot walk, but slides along, one leg bent under, the other stretched out. Her father lives with her in her house and lies there covered up with his tent. The dog lives at the door of her house.

Many people have speculated about the moral or message of this story. Some have suggested that Avilayoq's refusal to accept a husband put this tragedy in motion. Other storytellers have offered the idea that it was the mistreatment of Avilayoq that caused her to become Sedna, the bitter woman down below, who punishes those who break taboos. She is harsh in her punishments and shows no mercy, as none was shown to her.

Unikkaaqtuat

This version was recorded in the Netsilik region.

This version of the Mother of the Sea Mammals is included because it presents a very different beginning. Instead of a proud woman who would not accept a suitor, the Mother of the Sea Mammals is a mistreated orphan.

Traditional Inuit life was governed by many taboos. These varied region to region.

The Orphan Girl who Became the Mother of the Sea Mammals

Everything came from the ground. In the past, people lived on the ground. They ate rocks and dirt, as we now eat animals. But, back then, there were no animals to hunt. And people knew nothing of all the strict taboos that we have to observe now. For no dangers threatened them. On the other hand, no pleasures awaited them after a long day's toil.

Then one day, as people from a village were crossing a fiord in a raft made with kayaks tied together, a little orphan girl was pushed into the sea. It was just the same as with the thunder and lightning. Nobody cared about the orphan girl and, as she hid on the kayak-raft, she was pushed into the sea. But that wickedness turned her into a great spirit, the greatest of all the spirits. She became Nuliajuk and made the animals that we hunt. Now everything comes from her—everything that people love or fear—food and clothes, hunger and bad hunting, abundance or lack of caribou, seals, meat, and blubber.

Because of her, people have to forever think out all the taboos that make life difficult. For now people can no longer live eating rocks and dirt. Now we depend on timid and cunning animals.

The Woman who Married the Dog

This version was recorded in the South Baffin region

Unikkaaqtuat

This traditional story explains the origins of Inuit and other races. This story is occasionally connected to the story of the mother of the sea mammals, however, it is often told as a separate story.

At Padli there lived a man whose name was Apasinasee. He had a daughter who did not want to take a husband.

Finally, her father grew angry and said to her one evening, "You who do not want to take a husband, why not marry my dog?"

His daughter did not reply. Early in the morning, he spoke to her in the same way, but his daughter remained silent. The following night a man came into the hut who wore trousers of red dog skin. He sat down next to the girl and then lay down with her. He copulated with her and when he left the hut the next morning, he dragged her along, as dogs do. It was her father's dog that had assumed the shape of a man.

That day, the father said to his daughter, "Now you have a husband."

During the day the dog did not enter the house, but in the evening the same man with the dog-skin trousers appeared and sat down with the girl.

Thus they continued to live for some time, and the woman soon found herself with child. Eventually, her time came and she gave birth to a litter of young dogs. When they began to grow up, they made a great deal of noise and the woman's parents grew tired of them. Her father took the young woman, the pups, and the dog to a small island. He told the dog to come back across every day to fetch meat for his family. The young woman hung a pair of boots around his neck and, after her father had filled them with meat, the dog swam back to the island.

They continued to live in this manner for some time, but finally the old man became tired of supplying the young dogs with meat. One day, when the dog came across, he filled the boots with stones and covered the top with meat. The dog began to swim back, as he always did. But when he was halfway to the island the weight of the rocks began to pull him under. As he struggled, he cried out because he wanted to reach his wife and pups very badly. When the dog reached the bottom of the sea, Sedna took him into her house.

The woman was then all alone with her dogs on the island, and the old man went across regularly to supply her with seal meat. Finally, he complained to his daughter, saying that he was tired of supplying the pups with meat. She became angry and resolved to avenge the death of her husband.

She said to her pups, "When my father comes back, go down to the beach and lap the seal blood off the cover of his kayak. Then attack him and devour him."

When the father arrived, bringing meat for the pups, they ran down to the beach and lapped the blood off the cover of the kayak. The old man scolded them, and tried to drive them away. Then they attacked him and devoured him, as they had been told to do.

The woman felt sorry for her pups, because she had no food for them. She took the sole of one of her boots, made masts of whalebone and transformed it into a ship. She then gathered provisions for their journey.

Many versions tell us that this group became the ancestors of the Europeans.

She told some of her children to go aboard, and said, "Whatever country you may reach, you will make things beautiful for yourselves. You are crying for food all the time and I have nothing to give you."

When a fair wind from the north began to blow, she pushed the ship offshore and the pups sailed away over the ocean. It is not known to what place they went.

Then she sent off more of her children and said, "Go inland and live on caribou."

They became the Ijiqat. They are much larger than men and live on caribou only. She sent forth still another part of her brood and told them to go away.

"You may eat anything you find," she said to them.

They became the Inuarudligat. They are about as high as the knee of a man but are very strong and can drag a walrus up to their tent. They use the ears of a fox for their children's dress. The last of the brood stayed with the woman and became the ancestors of the Inuit.

This version was recorded in the South Baffin region.

In this etiological tale the origin of the walrus and the caribou are linked. In many traditional stories, intentions had the power of creation. This certainly seems the case in this story.

Origin of the Walrus and of the Caribou

A long time ago a woman transformed her old sealskin jacket into a walrus. She put antlers on its head and then put it into the water. It looked very convincing. Then she transformed her trousers into a caribou. The black part became the back of the animal, while the white part became its belly. The waistband was used to make its legs, and the connecting parts of the trousers were used to make its loins. Then she put tusks in its head. It looked very real, and she set it free. When the caribou saw a man, it walked up to him and killed him with its tusks. Then she called both the walrus and the caribou to come to her. She pulled the tusks out of the caribou's mouth and put them into the walrus's mouth. She took the antlers from the walrus and put them on the caribou's head. She also removed some of the caribou's teeth. Then she kicked its forehead so that it became flat and so that its eyes protruded. In this way she punished it for having killed the man.

Then she said to the caribou, "You shall never come near the walrus. Stay far away inland."

Ever since that time, whenever a caribou smells a man, it is afraid.

This version was recorded in the Kivalliq region.

Origin of the Caribou

A long time ago a spirit came to a village and married a woman. He did not need any food and did not go hunting. The men of the village told him repeatedly that he had to provide for his wife, and that he must go hunting. Finally, the spirit grew angry and with his spear made a hole in the ground. Out jumped a caribou, which he killed and took home. The next time he went to gather meat for his wife, a man from the village followed him secretly and saw how he caught the caribou and how he closed up the hole again. As soon as the spirit had gone back to the village, the villager opened the hole. He did not close it quickly enough and all the caribou came out and spread over the earth. When the spirit saw the caribou, he became angry. He kicked them in the forehead, so as to press the forehead flat, and told them to run away and to always fear man.

Origin of the Narwhal

This version was recorded the South Baffin region.

Although this story explains the origin of narwhal, it also cautions us on the dangers of mistreating those weaker than ourselves.

Once upon a time, there lived, north of Padli, a woman who had two stepchildren—a blind boy and a girl. One day a bear came to their house and looked in through the window. The mother gave a bow and arrow to the blind boy and aimed the arrow for him. Then she told him to shoot and he killed the bear.

He said, "Indeed, I have killed it."

The step-mother replied, "No, no, your arrow only struck the side of the window."

The blind boy heard the growling of the bear grow weaker and weaker, until the animal fell over and tumbled down from the roof of the house into the snow. The woman went out and skinned the bear, but she told the girl not to mention it to her brother. Although the woman had now plenty of meat, she kept the blind boy starving. The girl, when eating, would sometimes hide a piece of meat under her sleeve, in order to give it to her brother when her mother was absent.

One day the blind boy asked his sister, "Don't you see a pond not far away from here?"

"Yes," she replied, "I see a small lake."

"Are there any birds on it?"

"Yes, there are some."

"Then take me by the hand and lead me to the lake."

When they reached the lake, they saw two birds. The boy asked his sister to go home and leave him alone.

Soon the birds came ashore and one of them said to him, "Sit down on top of my kayak!"

He did so and the bird paddled away with him to the middle of the lake. Then suddenly the bird dove into the water with the boy and stayed below water for quite a while.

When they came up again, the boy found himself on top of the kayak, and the bird asked him, "Can you see now?"

He replied, "No, I cannot see."

But he could discern a shimmer of light. Then the bird dove with him again and stayed underwater much longer.

When they came to the surface, the bird asked him again, "Can you see now?"

The blind boy replied, "I can see better now, but not very well."

They dove again and stayed underwater still longer.

When they came up again, the bird asked him, "Can you see now?

Can you see that lake and the things that look like pins in the water?" The blind boy replied, "No, I cannot see them."

They dove once more and stayed underwater a very long time.

When they came up the bird asked once more, "Can you see those things like pins standing in the water?"

The blind boy replied, "Yes, I see them."

Then the bird took him ashore. The boy had very keen eyesight now.

He went to his mother's tent and saw a bearskin drying outside the house.

He said to his mother, "Where did you get that bearskin?"

She replied, "I got it from people who were passing in a boat."

He got his harpoon line and his other hunting implements ready and went to hunt white whales.

He said to his mother, "Won't you go with me? I am going to hunt white whales."

She agreed.

When they reached the floe edge, he said to his mother, "Make fast the end of the line around your waist, and hold on to it when I harpoon a white whale. You shall help me hold it."

Suddenly a white whale emerged. It was of a dark colour.

Then the woman shouted to her stepson, "Harpoon that one!"

But he replied, "No, it is too strong."

Quite a number of white whales emerged, but he waited until a very large one came near, then he speared it with his harpoon. He pretended to help his mother hold the line, but gradually he pushed her onto the edge of the floe and the whale pulled her under water.

When the whale came up again, the woman also rose to the surface. She cried and shouted to her stepson, "Don't you remember the time when I bathed you when you were a child?"

The white whale dove again and took the woman along.

Then the boy heard her crying, "Luk-luk!" and her head went under water.

When the whale came up again, the woman lay on her back. She took her hair in her hands and twisted it into the form of a horn.

Again she cried, "Oh, stepson! Why do you throw me into the water? Don't you remember that I bathed you when you were a child?"

She was transformed into a narwhal. Then the white whale and the narwhal swam away.

The boy returned to the shore. He left that place with his sister, and they went travelling for a long time. Finally they came upon a snow house. The boy built a house for the two of them nearby. Then he asked his sister to go into the other snow house and ask for a drink of water. The people in the snow house, who had very long fingernails, were afraid of the strangers.

The girl and her brother thought the people with the long fingernails were not real people. When the girl asked for a drink of water for her brother, one of them said to her, "Take off your jacket and take the water out of the bucket."

"Not real people" is an expression often seen in old translations. In these old stories, there is a reoccurring idea that sometimes beings might look like people, but they are not. They may be an animal pretending to be human or some kind of earth spirit.

She took off her jacket and her shirt. While she was reaching out to take some water, the people with the long fingernails scratched her until her skin was torn. She began to cry. When her brother heard her cries, he ran into the house and killed the people with his knife. The boy wrapped his sister in rabbit skins to cover her wounds and carried her on his back as they travelled.

After they had journeyed for a long time, he met some people, the Ikingan, who were very kind to them. By this time the girl's wounds had healed and she was able to walk again.

Ikingan were a race of beings that lacked anuses.

When the brother and sister reached the Ikingan's camp, these kind people were standing outside of their huts. The girl noticed a great deal of caribou fat lying about.

When she took up a piece and began to eat it, they cried out, "Don't eat that! It is dirt. Come into the hut, we have plenty of food there."

She went in and saw plenty of meat, of which she and her brother ate. She noticed that the people did not eat any meat, but just took a piece of fat, which they chewed and spit out again. These people had no anuses and had to regurgitate their waste.

The girl married one of these men. Soon, she was with child. One day her mother-in-law made some thread out of caribou sinew, which she plaited.

The girl's brother asked, "Why are you making that thread?"

The woman replied, "It is for your sister, to sew her up after they have taken out her child."

The young man said, "That is not necessary. She does not need to be sewed up; she can give birth by herself."

And the people were surprised to find that her child was born without her being cut open. It was a boy, and they were well pleased with it. They were especially excited that this child had an anus.

They asked the girl, "What are you going to call the child?"

And when one of the women replied, "Porlolee" ("Mittens"), the new mother misunderstood, believing that she was being asked to put on mittens.

The mother did not understand that this was to be the child's name. When the people saw that the child had an anus, they wanted to have one also. They put some sharpened pegs into the ground and sat down on them, thus forcing the pegs into their bodies: they made anuses for themselves. Only a few of the Ikingan died by the operation, but most were successful.

How the Narwhal Came

This version was recorded in Northern Greenland (Polar Inuit).

Unikkaaqtuat

This Greenlandic version of how the narwhal came to be is very similar to the South Baffin version that precedes this story. Many of the same Inuit traditional stories can be found, without much variation, across the circumpolar north.

Once upon a time, there was a man who could not see, and when his fellow villagers went out seal catching, they left him with his mother and his little sister.

One day, as the blind man lay asleep, his mother woke him.

"A bear, a bear in the window!" she said, and he strained his bow as she guided his hand.

"That sounded as if the bear was hit!" he cried, as the arrow fell.

"Oh no! You hit the windowsill."

She wanted to eat the entire bear herself—she gave her son only shellfish.

But his little sister let lumps of meat drop down under her fur collar and gave them to her brother.

One day, in the middle of summer, the blind man said to his sister:

"Lead me up to a lake."

She guided him up to a lake. As he stood there by the lake, a loon came and began to speak.

"Take hold of me round my neck, I will carry you!" it said. Then it dove down into the sea with him. The blind man very nearly drowned. The loon began to dive into the lake with the man over and over again. When they finally surfaced, the blind man gasped for breath.

"Do you see land?" asked the loon.

"I see!" shouted the man, but the loon dove again, and then again.

"Do you see now?"

"I see wide countries!"

And then the man had his sight again. When he went home he noticed a bearskin spread out near his hut.

"A bearskin spread out!" exclaimed the man, when he arrived home. He was surprised to see the skin, as his mother had told him he had shot only the windowsill.

"One that has been left by Persoqaq," lied his mother.

"Look, look, white whales in sight!" said the man as he looked out over the water.

"Harpoon them! Harpoon them! And bind me fast to the line!" said the mother, eagerly. And so he fastened her to the line.

"Choose the little one, I can manage that," called out the mother, and so he threw the harpoon at a little white whale.

The next day he decided to put an end to his mother's life as revenge for how he had been treated. Again he fastened her to the harpoon line, but this time he chose a very large white whale, which was too strong for his mother to hold, and she was dragged into the sea.

"My curved knife, my curved knife!" cried the mother, as she was about to disappear in the waves. She wanted to cut the line but he did not throw her the knife. His mother did not come back and was changed into a narwhal, for she plaited her hair into tusks and from her the narwhals are descended. Before her, there were only white whales.

The man grieved that he had killed his mother and went away with his sister. On their travels they came to people with long claws. These people had no knives, but used their claws to flay and cut up animals.

"Let them come in," said the oldest of them.

When the two had gone in, they tore the man's sister to pieces and ate her.

"Why are you eating her?" the man cried out in anger. Then he killed them with a walrus tusk. He collected his sister's bones, put them

Note the increased level of violence in this story compared to the previous version. In the other version is girl is only injured, here she is killed and eaten.

in a bag, and carried them away.

This man was a great magician and as he carried his sister on his back, she began gradually to come to life again. At last, she began to talk:

"Brother, let me become well," she said. Then she began to grow heavy to carry.

Eventually they came to people again, people without anuses. Among them the brother took a wife and the sister a husband. The brother and sister settled down among these people for good, had children, and grew old.

Unikkaaqtuat

Although this story was recorded in the South Baffin region, it is likely that the storyteller was from the Kivalliq or Kitikmeot region as there are no grizzly bears on Baffin Island.

This creation story is one of mistreatment and its consequence. The cruelty of parents motivates a helpless daughter to become powerful.

Origin of the Agdlaq

O nce upon a time, a man, his wife, and his two daughters lived in a snow house. For some reason the father disliked his elder daughter and made up his mind to murder her. He built a snow house for her and closed the door with a snow block. He intended to let her starve to death, but her younger sister, who loved her, made a small hole through the wall of the snow house and passed pieces of seal meat to her.

After some time, the elder sister said, when the younger one was giving seal meat to her, "I am not like other people. Hair is growing all over my body and on my limbs."

After a while, the elder sister also said to her, "Do not bring me any more meat."

The younger sister replied, "I shall continue to bring you meat, for I want you to live."

Soon the father and mother discovered the girl giving seal meat to her elder sister. The father said, "It is not acceptable that you give her food. She is not nice. It is best to let her die. Do not give her any more food."

But the girl insisted on giving some of her own seal meat to her elder sister.

One day, when she took seal meat to her elder sister, she looked into the house through the hole and saw that her sister's body was covered with hair.

The elder sister knew at once that the girl had seen her and she said, "Leave this place! I shall soon get out of this snow house."

She made a number of wooden pegs and gave them to her younger sister, saying, "When you move from this place, you will hear something pursuing you while you are travelling. Lie down on your face and put these pegs around you. I am going to turn into an agdlaq. I shall pursue you, but by the pegs I shall recognize you."

About this time, the father decided to desert his elder daughter. The family loaded their sledges and left. When they had been on their way for some time, the girl heard something following their steps. She ran ahead, lay down on the snow, put the wooden pegs around her, as she had been told to do by her sister, and hid her face in her hands.

She stayed there for some time. Soon the agdlaq came up to her, but when it saw the pegs it turned back. After some time she looked up, and she found that her father and mother had been killed by the monster. Her elder sister, who had been transformed into an agdlaq, had killed them.

"Agdlaq" is the Inuktitut word for grizzly bear.

This version was recorded in the South Baffin region.

There are several stories that explain how various constellations came to be. The following is one such story.

The Hunters that Transformed into a Constellation

Once upon a time, a bear was being hunted by seven sledges. The traces of a number of dogs had been cut, and the dogs were in hot pursuit. When they came up close to the bear, some of the men jumped off their sledges and ran, urging the dogs along.

One man shouted to another, "Your mitten has fallen off of the sledge! Go and get it! You can see it by the moon's light!"

While the sledges were thus hurrying along, one of the men said, "I do not feel my feet touching the ground."

And another one replied, "The runners of my sledge are rising."

They were transferred to the sky and became constellations.

The Akla that Turned into Fog

This version was recorded in the Kivalliq region.

There was once an akla, a land bear, which lived in human form. It used to go down to the dwellings of men and steal away dead bodies. Sometimes it would also take live human beings. One day a man pretended to be dead and laid himself down in a grave. The akla came and stole him away and carried him home with him.

In the early days, animals often spoke and had the ability to shape-shift. Some chose to live in human form. This was the case for a family of barren ground grizzly. Even though they chose to live in human form, they scavenged carrion as a grizzly would. In this story, quick thinking and resourcefulness saves an Inuit hunter and protects his village. This story also explains the origin of fog.

The man was carried with his head pointing downward, and every time they passed any bushes on the way, he grabbed hold of the bushes so that the akla had to exert all its strength to move along. The akla arrived at its house and laid the man up on the side bench, head downward, to thaw. But the akla itself was now so tired that it at once lay down on the bed to rest.

"Father, the 'meat' is opening its eyes!" cried the akla's children.

"Well, let it open them. Today it grabbed hold of all the bushes we passed, so it was a hard job to get it home."

But the man, who had pretended to be a corpse, sprang up, took an axe, and killed the akla.

The akla's wife was in the cooking place and when the man entered he saw a human skin filled with human fat. The man ran and cut a hole in the skin so that the fat ran out and the akla's wife—not wanting to lose the fat—frantically tried to save as much of it as she could. Despite this attempt to delay her, the akla's wife soon set off after the man and caught up to him. When she was close to him, he drew a line on the ground with his middle finger and at once a great, fiercely rushing river sprang out from the ground.

"How did you get over?" cried the akla's wife.

"I swallowed it down and emptied it," cried the man.

Then the akla's wife lay down and drank and drank until she burst; when she burst, all the water she had drunk rose up in a mist over the earth and became fog. And it is from her that the fog comes.

Origin of Fog

This version was recorded in the South Baffin region.

Nareya was a huge man who lived in the interior of the country. When running down caribou, he bound his body with thongs to prevent himself from running too fast, and to steady his belly, which was enormous. He overtook the caribou easily and knocked them down with stones. He would eat the meat of three caribou at one meal. He was a glutton and a cannibal, even robbing graves for an easy meal. After meals, he would go to the river, where he had a place scooped out large enough for his belly. He would lie down and drink of the water until he had enough. He would lie there until he felt hungry again.

This version of how fog came includes the character of Nareya, a huge man. He is reputed to be a great glutton with a huge belly that needs to be lashed when he hunts. Other than Nareya, this version of the origin of fog is quite similar to the previous story.

One day a man who was out caribou hunting came to the place at the side of the river where Nareya was lying. The man watched him for a long time, until finally Nareya looked up and saw him. Nareya arose at once and ran after the man, who tried to escape. Nareya overtook him and killed him. When the hunter did not return to the village, his friends became very anxious and one of them went in search of him.

His friend did not find the hunter, but, on his return, he discovered that the bodies of the dead had been taken away from the graves. Finally, he came to the place where Nareya was lying, at the side of the water.

Then he went home and told what he had seen. The people did not know what to do. One of them offered to pretend to be dead and to have himself buried under stones. He expected that he would be taken away, like the bodies of the dead, and that he would thus discover the grave robber. The people carried the volunteer out of the house and covered him up with stones. When it was nearly morning, Nareya discovered the new grave. He took the stones off, fastened a thong around the body in two places, put it on his back, and carried it away. When he got home, he took off the rope and put the body down.

The man, who was an angakkuq, pretended to be dead; but when he thought nobody was looking, he blinked with his eyes and saw Nareya, Nareya's wife, and Nareya's child in the tent. The man knew that this was the thief who had been taking away the bodies of his friends. He thought that Nareya must have also killed the caribou hunter. He heard Nareya explain how he had eaten three caribou in a single day. Nareya told his wife to make a fire and to cook the body. While the woman started the fire, the child thought he noticed the eyes of the man moving.

He said so, but Nareya replied, "Nevermind."

"Yesterday, when I brought the body here, it seemed to be very heavy."

Nareya turned to his wife and asked, "Is the water hot?"

When she answered in the affirmative, the man jumped up and knocked Nareya down. Then he ran away as fast as he could.

Soon Nareya recovered and pursued him. The man distracted Nareya's attention by means of sorcery. Nareya stopped for a time, but soon continued his pursuit. When Nareya had nearly reached the man, the latter used his sorcery to create many berries. When Nareya saw them, he stopped to pick and eat a great many. Meanwhile, the man ran over a hill. When he reached the foot of the hill, and saw the monster gaining upon him, he made a river.

Nareya reached the river and asked the man, who was on the other side, "How did you cross?"

The man replied, "I drank all the water until I was able to wade through the river."

Then Nareya lay down and began to drink. He almost emptied the river, then went across it, and, when he came to the other side, shook the water out of his sleeves. His stomach was so full of water that as he shook he burst and died. A mist arose from him and from it all the mist and fog originated. The man lost his way in the fog, but after some time it cleared away and he reached home safely.

Origin of the Red Phalarope and of the Web-footed Loon

This version was recorded in the South Baffin region.

In this tale, a boy and his grandmother escape hardship and are transformed into birds.

Katsu, an old woman, had an adopted son. One day, while the boy was out in his kayak, there arose a strong breeze from the shore. The boy paddled hard for shore, but could not reach it. For three days he struggled against the wind.

The old woman ran up and down the beach, crying, "Grandson, paddle, paddle harder!"

His face became quite red from the effort of paddling and blood, from this nose, began to stream over the front of his clothing.

Still, the old woman continued to shout to him, "Grandson, paddle, paddle, paddle harder! I have no other boy. Paddle harder!" And then she burst into tears, wailing, "Ah, ah, ah! Ah, ah, ah, kayalau!"

She wore long boots, and as she walked up and down the beach, the soles of her feet began to turn upward. The boy's strength gave out and he began to drift away. He was transformed into a phalarope. The woman kept on walking until the soles of her boots were completely turned up, and her clothing was covered with blood. She was transformed into a loon.

The Ptarmigan

This version was recorded in the South Baffin region

This story begins with a little boy who refuses to fall asleep.

"Grandmother, tell me a story!" the little boy asked.

"Go to sleep, I have no story," replied his grandmother.

"Grandmother, tell me a story!" the little boy said again.

"From there, from there, from the little corner of the tent, came a little lemming that had no hair at all, that went under a person's armpit."

The grandmother tickled the boy, and he turned into a bird, then flew away.

His grandmother called out, "Grandson, grandson! Where is he, where is he?"

The child and his grandmother became ptarmigans. The peculiar cry of these birds is interpreted as "Nauk, aauk" ("Where, where?") which is an imitation of the grandmother's cry. The red mark over the eye of the ptarmigan is said to be the result of the grandmother's weeping for her grandson.

This cautionary tale for children explains what happened to a child who refused to listen to his grandmother.

"Grandmother, tell me a story" is the quintessential way in which storytelling was initiated.

This version is from the South Baffin region.

The Ptarmigan and the Snow Bunting

One evening a boy asked his grandmother to tell him a story; but she only replied, "Go to bed and sleep. I have no story to tell."

Then the boy began to cry and insisted that she tell him a story.

The old woman began to rock herself from side to side.

"I will tell you a story. I will tell you a long story about the lemming without hair that was in that place on the porch there. It wanted to stay under my arm to keep warm. It had no hair and it cried when it jumped up to go to its bed, 'Too, too, too!'"

The boy became frightened and ran away. He was transformed into a snow bunting. The old woman searched for him everywhere but could not find him. Finally she gave up looking and sat down to cry. The tears ran down her face and she kept rubbing her eyes until they became quite red and the skin came off. She had a small skin bag which she put on her chest, close to her neck. She became a ptarmigan.

The Ptarmigan and the Small Bird

This version is from the Kivalliq region.

A long time ago an old woman lived with her child in a snow house. One night the child said to his grandmother, "Grandmother, tell me a story."

"I don't know any story. Go to sleep!"

Wishing to frighten the child, she said, "Oh! I see a lemming without hair. And there's another one and still another one!"

Then she gave a jump as though she were afraid of these imaginary lemmings. At the same time she gave a scream.

This frightened the child so much that he curled himself up so small that he became a small bird and flew away in terror. His grandmother felt sorry at the loss of her child.

"Now, now, now!" she cried and wailed. She rubbed her eyes so that the skin came off around the lids. She hung a pouch around her neck and put her needle into the leg of her boot. Then she flew away and became a ptarmigan. The pouch became her gizzard, while the needle became the bone of her leg.

Unikkaaqtuat

The Wind

This version was recorded in the Kivalliq region.

This story is about Narrsuk, a giant who lives in the sky and makes wind and storms. A more complete version of this story is presented in Kappianaqtut: Strange Creatures and Fantastic Beings from Inuit Myths and Legends (Volume 1).

"The Wind is a being in the form of a person" is referring to the belief that everything has an anthropomophic representation of its essence (Inua). In this case the storyteller is referring to the orphaned giant, Narrsuk. This giant is somtimes called, Sila, which is also the Inuktitut word for sky and weather.

The wind is a being in the form of a person. When he feels warm, he opens his coat and the wind escapes. The only way to make the wind stop is for an angakkuq to go to the wind spirit, fasten his coat, and cross his arms. Only then will the wind subside. The Netsilik say that one of their angakkuit once went to see the wind spirit and threatened to kill him with a knife. The wind spirit replied that he would level everything on earth. The angakkuq did not believe him and asked him to show his power by destroying a certain mountain. The wind spirit at once pushed it over with his foot. Then the angakkuq believed him and never questioned the wind's power again.

The Loon and the Raven

This version is from the Kivalliq region.

Since both the loon and the raven were good dressmakers, they agreed to make a suit of clothes for each other. They sewed the skins together with thread which they rubbed with lampblack. The raven took the needle first and weaved it in and out of the skin on which she was working until the seam had gone all round the loon's body. This is why the loon is speckled.

Then the loon took the needle and commenced work on the raven. But the latter would not sit still, and at last the loon lost patience and poured the contents of the lamp over the raven, thus making her black all over. The raven became angry, took a stone, and threw it at the loon, thus breaking her legs and making them flat.

Mistreatment and Consequence

In this chapter, the stories give detailed descriptions about the abuse of certain community members, almost invariably an orphan, and the fearful consequences of such actions.

The reader may want to be on the lookout for the following:

- ⊙ *The appearance of vulnerable orphans*
- ⊙ *Bad treatment that is often unmotivated*
- ⊙ *Envy*
- ⊙ *Intervention*
- ⊙ *Revenge*
- ⊙ *Unresolved endings*
- ⊙ *Disrespect for traditions and consequences*

Qaudjaqdjuq

Once upon a time, there was a boy named Qaudjaqdjuq. He had no father and no mother. His only friend was the Man in the Moon. The people in his village treated him badly. He had to fetch salt water for them, not between the ground ice but from the floe edge. He had to carry the water in an animal bladder. He had no mittens, although he had to bring the water such a long distance.

One time, when he had been sent out for water, the ice broke and he went adrift. After drifting for a long time, the ice carried him back to the shore, where there was a village. There he fared no better than he had before. The people made him sleep on the porch, with the dogs, and when the men and women went in and out they stepped on his hands and feet. They made him clean the lamps and pots with his clothes. One day, when Qaudjaqdjuq was all alone, he said, "Brother Moon, up there, come down to me in the morning." Very soon the Moon came down, along with his dog team and his wife.

There was a large dancing house, built of stone, in the village. The

This version was recorded in the South Baffin region.

Inuit stories commonly feature orphans.

This story introduces the reader to the Moon man. This being often comes to the rescue of the mistreated.

In other versions of this story, it is the orphan's older brother that comes to his rescue.

people assembled there every night. They had one large chamber pot in this dancing house, and it was Qaudjaqdjuq's duty to empty the pot whenever required. He was unable to carry it with his hands alone; he had to hold it with his teeth also. When he was done emptying the pot, the people used to hang him from a pair of walrus tusks by his nostrils, which made his nostrils extremely large. The Man in the Moon and his wife went with the people into the dancing house where Qaudjaqdjuq was hanging from the tusks. After some time, the people told the boy to take out the chamber pot again. Then the Man in the Moon said to Qaudjaqdjuq, "Let me try. I will take it outside for you." But the Man in the Moon upset the pot, and the urine ran all over the floor. The people grew angry. They left Qaudjaqdjuq and the Man in the Moon alone in the house, and walled up the doorway with large boulders.

The Man in the Moon asked the boy to bring in the seat from his sledge. The boy went to the door of the dancing house and asked one of the people to hand him the seat. Although the people were still engaged in walling up the doorway, one of them passed the seat to the boy. There was a dead ermine in the seat. The Man in the Moon brought the creature to life; then it ran out between the boulders. As soon as the people saw the ermine, they ran after it and, in their eagerness of pursuit, they stumbled over one another, and one of the men was killed.

The ermine ran back into the dancing house. The bristles around its mouth were covered with blood. After a short time, the Man in the Moon sent the animal out again. Again the people pursued it and, in their eagerness, fell over each other and another person was killed. The ermine escaped into the dancing house again; the Moon Man saw that its mouth was covered with still more blood. Then the ermine dug away the earth from under the boulders that blocked the doorway and the Man in the Moon and Qaudjaqdjuq were able to get out.

The two walked some distance from the village. They were very careful not to leave any tracks behind, lest the people know where they had gone. When they were all alone, the Man in the Moon said to Qaudjaqdjuq, "I am going to whip you and when I ask you, 'Do you feel sore?' you must answer, 'No, I am not sore'." The Man in the Moon took up his whip and whipped the boy until he fell down.

Then he asked him, "Do you feel sore, brother?"

Qaudjaqdjuq replied, "No, I am not sore."

The boy arose again, and the Man in the Moon whipped him a second time until the boy fell down.

Again he asked him, "Do you feel sore?"

Qaudjaqdjuq replied in the same way as before. Suddenly the boy was much larger. The Man in the Moon whipped him a third time and asked him the same question; Qaudjaqdjuq replied that he did not feel sore at all. This time he did not fall over after he had been whipped. Again the boy grew larger. Thus the Man in the Moon whipped him six times and the boy became a very large and strong man.

The Man in the Moon then wished for three bears to visit the village. It did not take long for the bears to come.

When the people saw them, they were afraid and said, "Where is Qaudjaqdjuq? Let us give him to the bears to feed on."

They did not know that Qaudjaqdjuq had become a strong man.

After they had called him several times, Qaudjaqdjuq replied, "Here is the little boy."

He came down to the huts, and the people were surprised when they saw him.

They shouted, "Qaudjaqdjuq is a large man now!"

Qaudjaqdjuq went down to the bears. He took one of them by its hind-legs, struck it against the ground, and killed it. The second and the third bear fared no better. Then the people were very afraid of Qaudjaqdjuq and they ran away in all directions. But he pursued them and, as soon as he overtook a man, he picked him up, struck him against the rocks, and killed him.

When he grabbed hold of each man, he would say, "Do you remember when you made me clean your dirty lamps and when you made me empty your dirty pots and when you hung me by my nostrils from the tusks? Have you forgotten how you threw a piece of walrus head at me, as you would at a dog? How you gave me no knife with which to cut?"

But there were two women in the village whom Qaudjaqdjuq liked. He used to clean their lamps best. He asked them to become his wives, but the women said to him, "You used to make all your clothes dirty wiping our lamps."

He retorted, "My clothes are very nice now," although he still wore the same suit that he had used when he was a poor little boy.

The two women quickly replied to him, but one of them was quicker than the other. Qaudjaqdjuq squeezed the slower one just a little, but he did not know his own strength and he hurt her very much.

Later, Qaudjaqdjuq said to his wives, "Light that stick and give it to me."

One of the women was very fast, while the other one did not give him the stick at once. He struck the slower woman on the shoulder. He always found this woman slow and, on account of being struck so often on her left side, her left shoulder became lower than her right one. The other woman began to squint in her right eye because she was always looking stealthily in Qaudjaqdjuq's direction, anxious of his anger.

The consequence of mistreatment is a common theme in Inuit stories. And, often, even after the abusers have been punished, the cruel experiences suffered by the victim cause them to become cruel adults.

This version was recorded in the South Baffin region.

The Boy who Harpooned a Whale

At Niutang, in Kingnait, there was an orphan boy. One day the people were in a house eating whale skin. The boy cut off a tough part of skin and said to the owner of the house:

"People say that it is difficult to drive a harpoon through the skin of the whale. It is not tough at all. It is very soft and tender."
The boy did not know, however, that the owner had missed a whale that day.

The man, thinking that the boy was making fun of him, became angry, and said, "Next time we go whaling, you will have to be harpooneer."

The boy replied, "I do not know how to harpoon whales."
But the man insisted.

After some time, when the weather was fair, he said to the boy, "Come, we will go whaling today."

But the boy retorted, "My muscles are not strong enough yet."
He was compelled to go along, however.

"Come," said the man, "you know that the whale skin is not tough. You said so the other day. You think it is soft and tender. You think that it is easy to drive a harpoon through it."

The boat was manned and they went off. The boy was seated in the centre of the boat, next to the man who had compelled him to go along. After some time, they saw a whale, but it did not come near enough. Then a very large whale arose. The boy was told to go ahead and throw his harpoon. He crawled under the thwarts to the bow of the boat. He stood erect and took up the harpoon and when he did this he looked like a strong man. He waved his hand to the steersman to turn the boat a little. Then he raised his harpoon and when he looked back the others saw that his face looked like a man's face and that he had a beard. He threw his harpoon deep into the whale's body and then crawled back to his place. When he arrived back at his seat in the boat he looked like a boy again.

The men in their kayaks were ready to lance the whale when it rose again, but when it came up, they found that it was dead.

All the men said, "We have never before seen a boy kill a whale."

They towed it ashore and talked about the boy who, although so small, had killed a whale with one thrust of his harpoon. It took days to cut up the carcass because the whale was so large.

The boy's ending comments are not meant to be derogatory towards woman; rather, he acknowledges his inexperience and immaturity.

Many months later, the boy said, "I use only a whale bone knife when I eat whale meat, because it is so tender." Some time after this, when he was larger, he said, "I am still like a woman. I can only go out and sit about. I am not a man yet, although I harpooned a whale when I was a little boy."

The Artificial Skull that Frightened People to Death

There once lived at Kingawa five families and an old woman and her grandchild. They were all neighbours, yet all of the families except for one were unkind to this old woman. All the unkind and ungenerous families would give her to eat was the backbone or hindquarters, after all the good meat had been cut off, which the old woman would boil. In this way she lived for a long time. Once in a while her only friend would get a seal and then they would have a nice time, and she would be cheered up for a while.

Finally, the old woman resolved to take revenge on her ungenerous neighbours. Out of bones she made a form like a human skull, which she marked with soot. At dawn, shortly before the people left their houses, she placed the form near the door of one of the huts. When the people came out, they nearly died of fright. After one family had all come out and seen it, she moved it to another door. First one person and then another would come out, and, on seeing the skull, would almost die of fright. From that time on, they treated her more kindly and gave her meat with the bones.

The old woman finally took down the skull she had made and made another, larger one. After some time the people moved away. Then she sent the large skull after them. When they saw it, they all died. Her friends, however, did not desert her.

Papik

This version was recorded in Northern Greenland (Polar Inuit).

There was, once upon a time, a man whose name was Papik; he used to go seal catching with his brother-in-law, Ailaq. But it happened with these two that Ailaq always brought home seals, while Papik always returned empty handed. Each day Papik's envy grew.

Then one day Ailaq did not come back and Papik had no explanation for Ailaq's whereabouts when he returned home.

At last, late in the evening, Ailaq's mother rose and spoke—

"You have killed Ailaq!"

"No! I did not kill him," replied Papik.

"You have killed Ailaq!" she repeated, with raised voice.

"No! I did not kill him."

Then the old woman stood up and called out, "You have kept the murder secret. The day will come when I will eat you alive; for it was you who killed Ailaq!"

The old woman then prepared herself to die; for it was as a

Revenant is a ghost, a dead person that has come back.

revenant that she meant to avenge Ailaq. She drew her bearskin rug over herself and sat down on the beach near the tideway and let the flood rise over her.

For a long time after that, Papik did not go hunting, for he was afraid of the old woman's threat; but eventually he forgot about it and went seal hunting as usual.

One morning, two men stood on the ice by the side of a seal's breathing hole; a little way off, Papik had selected a place by himself. And then it happened: they heard a crackling in the snow, in Papik's direction, and a fog fell over the ice. Soon they heard the shrieks of a terrified man. A monster had attacked Papik.

Then they fled towards land. On their way they met sledges that were going out seal catching. They flung out their baggage and persuaded these other catchers to turn back to the village, so that they might not be frightened to death. In the village, all gathered together into one house. But when they heard the monster approaching on the ice outside, they rushed to the entrance. There was a great panic in the house as everyone pushed toward the door at once, and in the confusion an orphan boy was pushed. He fell backward into a tub filled with seal blood. When he got outside again, the blood poured down from him and everywhere he went he left a red mark in the snow.

"We shall certainly be food for the monster, now that the silly boy is marking our path with blood!" they called out.

"Let us kill him!" one proposed, but the others had compassion for the boy and let him live.

The evil spirit then came into view on the ice; they could only see its ears over the hummocks of ice as it crept along the bottom of the ice-hill. The spirit had taken the form of a bear. When it got up to the houses, not a single dog barked and not one dared to attack the spirit, for it was not a real bear.

But an old woman of the village spoke to the dogs, "See, your cousin has come; bark at him!

This released the dogs from their enchantment and they surrounded the bear. The men harpooned it.

But when they came to flay and cut up the bear, they recognized the old woman's rug in its skin; its bones were human bones.

The sledges then drove out to fetch the belongings they had left on the ice, and they found everything rent. When they discovered Papik, he was torn all to pieces. His eyes, his nose, his ears, his mouth, his vitals were all torn away, and he had been scalped.

And that is how the old woman avenged her son, Ailaq.

As our fathers used to say: when anyone kills a fellow creature without reason, a monster will attack him, frighten him to death, and not leave a limb of his corpse whole.

This story was told by the people who came from the other side of the sea.

Pautusôrssuaq, who Murdered his Uncle

This version was recorded in Northern Greenland (Polar Inuit).

There lived at Keikat a woman who was very beautiful; she was the wife of Alattaq. In the same village lived Pautusôrssuaq, who was Alattaq's nephew. He too was married, but he was fonder of his uncle's wife than of his own. The two therefore constantly exchanged wives, as people are in the habit of doing.

But one day late in the spring, Alattaq was about to start on a long seal-catching journey and decided to take his wife with him. They were standing down by the ice and just getting ready to leave when Alattaq's nephew came down to them.

"Are you going to leave us?" he asked.

"Yes, we are!" replied Alattaq.

When Pautusôrssuaq heard that his uncle would be taking his beautiful wife away with him, he rushed at Alattaq and killed him, for Pautusôrssuaq could not bear to see the woman he was so fond of leave.

When Pautusôrssuaq's wife saw that he had killed his uncle, she

Inland dwellers are supernatural beings often mentioned in traditional stories from Greenland.

An auk is a small, heavy-bodied seabird.

seized her sewing needle and thimble and fled away in the shadow of the tents, up over the cliffs to Eta, where her parents lived. She left with such haste that she forgot about a little boy she had been caring for and she left him sleeping in her tent. She had not even time to put on her stockings and so her feet grew very sore with running over the cliffs. On her way, she saw people inland, running about with loose hats on their heads, as the inland dwellers do. When these people saw her, they ran away so she could not speak to them.

Near Eta she caught sight of an old man, went up to him, and discovered that he was her father. He was out collecting little auks; they went home happily together to his tent.

After Pautusôrssuaq had killed his uncle, he rushed up to his tent to murder his wife; but she had fled already. He saw the little boy sitting in the tent where his wife had left him.

He fell upon the boy and said, "But where is she? Where has she run to?"

"I saw nothing. I was asleep!" lied the boy, for he was afraid. So Pautusôrssuaq was obliged to give up the attempt to catch his wife.

He took Alattaq's woman as his wife and lived with her. Soon she became a mother and gave birth to a monster with a large beard. She was so frightened by it that she died. He had received no pleasure from the woman he had stolen.

In the early summer many people had assembled at Natsilivik, on the way to Cape York. Among them was Pautusôrssuaq. One day a remarkable thing happened to him. When he was out seal catching, a fox set his teeth fast in the lappet of his coat and Pautusôrssuaq, thinking it an ordinary fox, swung at it, but could not hit it. It turned out that this fox was actually the soul of the murdered Alattaq. Alattaq's amulet was a fox, you see.

A lappet is a loose fold or flap of fabric on a piece of clothing.

Inuit used amulets for protection.

A short time afterward, Pautusôrssuaq was torn to pieces by Alattaq's spirit, in the shape of a bear. His daughter, who happened to be outside at that time, heard the shrieks and went in to tell the others, but as soon as she got inside, she forgot what she wanted to say, because the avenging spirit had conjured forgetfulness upon her.

It was only later that she remembered, and then it was too late. They found Pautusôrssuaq, torn limb from limb; they could see that he had tried to defend himself with great lumps of ice, but it had been of no avail.

That is how revenge comes upon people who murder.

The Wife-changers

This version was recorded in Northern Greenland (Polar Inuit).

Unikkaaqtuat

Once upon a time, there were two men, Talilarssuaq and Navssarssuaq, who exchanged wives. Talilarssuaq was a malicious fellow, who was very fond of frightening people.

One evening, as he was lying by the side of the woman he had borrowed, he took his long knife and drove it into the skin lying on the bed. Frightened, the woman ran away to her husband and said, "Go in and kill Talilarssuaq! He is lying there pretending to be dangerous!"

So, Navssarssuaq rose up, without saying a word. He dressed himself in his newest clothes, took his knife, and went out. He went straight to Talilarssuaq, who was still lying naked on the sleeping place talking to himself. Navssarssuaq dragged Talilarssuaq down on the floor and stabbed him until he was half dead.

"You might at least have waited until I had got my trousers on," said Talilarssuaq.

But Navssarssuaq dragged him out through the passage, flung him out on to the dung heap, and went his way in silence.

On the way home he met his wife.

"Are you going to kill me, too?" she asked. She was angry at her husband because he had taken Talilarssuaq's wife as his own.

"No!" he replied in a deep voice, "Pualuna is not big enough yet to do without you." Pualuna was their youngest son.

Some time after the murder, Navssarssuaq began to notice that he was followed about by a spirit.

"It is an invisible something that sometimes catches hold of me," he told the villagers. It was the avenging spirit keeping watch on him.

Just about that time, many in the village fell ill, and among them was Navssarssuaq. The sickness killed him, and so the avenging spirit had no opportunity to tear him to pieces.

This version was recorded in Northern Greenland (Polar Inuit).

The Man who did not Observe Taboos

There was once a man whose name was Artuk. He had just buried his dead wife under the stones, but he refused to observe the taboos that are imposed on those who have handled corpses. He did not believe in the precepts of his forefathers, he said.

Some of the people in the settlement were engaged in cutting up frozen meat for food. After he watched them cut up the meat with knives, he took a stone axe and chopped the meat up.

He said, "Look, that is the way to chop meat."

And he did this, although being a man who had touched a corpse, he was not allowed to cut meat.

The same day he went out on the ice and shook his undergarment free of lice, although he was forbidden to shake off vermin on the ice when he had just handled a dead body.

He also went up an ice cliff and drank water that had been melted by the sun, although he knew that it was forbidden to him.

He did all this to show defiance at what his countrymen believed. It was all lies, he said.

An ice cliff is frozen fresh water, really an iceberg before it becomes detached. When the sun melts the surface into little pools, the drinking-water obtained from it is delicious.

But one day, as he was about to start out with his sledge, fear came upon him. He dared not drive on the ice alone, and as his son would not accompany him of his own free will, he bound him to the uprights of his sledge and took him with him.

He never returned alive from that drive.

Late in the evening his daughter heard the mocking laughter of two spirits out in the air. She understood at once that they were laughing so she would know her father had paid the penalty of his transgressions.

The next day several sledges went out to look for Artuk. They found him a long way out on the ice, torn to pieces. Those who do not believe in the traditions of their fathers are always ripped asunder by the spirits.

The son, who was fast bound to the sledge, they had not touched. He had, however, died of fright.

This version was recorded in the South Baffin region.

The Emigration to the Land Beyond the Sea

There were a number of families living at Qenertung, and others at Ixa'luin, near Ixaluaqdjung, not far from Qenertung. In the spring, the people of Qenertung used to move to Operniving to hunt seals. In Qenertung lived a man and his wife who had a young son. The woman's mother also lived with them. The man was the only hunter at their camp. After some time the people from Ixa'luin moved to Qenertung and put up their huts there. Then all the men went out sealing together. At noon they took a bite of the seals that had been caught.

They lived in this way for some time, when one day the man who had been at Qenertung all winter caught a seal, a small portion of which he gave to the other men. In the evening, he cut it up in his hut and invited them to partake more of it. Some of the men remained outside, while one of them assisted in carving the seal. Suddenly, the host saw that the trouser legs of his companion were shaking and this frightened him. When the seal was all cut up, he went outside to wash his hands with snow. Then one of the other men jumped up and tried to throw him to the ground, but was unable to do so. The attacker called for assistance. The person who had helped cut the seal came out of the hut, took the man whom they were attacking by the feet, and threw him down on the ice. Then he killed him with his knife and they dragged the body away from the hut.

The murderer forced the man's widow to sleep with him. Early in the morning he went back to his own house, but every night he returned to the widow of the murdered man and slept with her.

One day she said to her mother, "My son would be able to kill that man if I were to hold him fast."

Her mother agreed. Then the woman told her son to kill their enemy when the opportunity arose. The boy was afraid to kill the man, but his mother urged him on until he consented.

The boy's grandmother said to him, "You do not need to be afraid. You can easily escape from them. We shall leave as soon as he is killed, while it is dark, and we shall be far away before they know anything about it. If they catch up with us, I can cut the ice and set it adrift."

Then his mother told him what to do.

In the evening the man came into the house again. The woman pretended to be in love with him and embraced him. When he lay on her, she held him with her arms and her legs. Then the boy took his knife and stabbed him from behind. As soon as he was dead, they harnessed their dogs to their sledges and started off. They were far out to sea before the people discovered the murder and started in pursuit. The dogs of the pursuers, however, went much faster than those of the woman and her family. The villagers soon began to catch up with the fugitives.

The old woman was lying on the sledge and did not notice the approach of the villagers.

The boy was afraid and began to cry, "Where is the one who promised to break the ice when our pursuers were gaining on us?"

Then the old woman raised her head and said, "I am here, my boy."

The dogs of the pursuers caught up to them. Then the old woman raised her bare hand and extended only her little finger, which she moved as though she were drawing a line between the two sledges. As she moved it, the ice broke and drifted away; fog rose from out of the water and they were safe from their pursuers. The old woman told the boy to stop driving the dogs, as they were now out of danger. They drifted about for some time, but finally reached the opposite side of the sea. There, they built a hut.

Every day the old woman went outside to look for other people.

Finally she met a man, who came to her and entered the house. He asked her to marry him and she consented. After some time she gave birth to a girl. The old woman and the man had been talking of making a kayak. One day the man found a piece of driftwood, which he buried in the damp sand on the beach. After a while, when he went to take the wood out, he found that it had grown and was suddenly very large. It was enough for the framework of a boat.

He began to build a kayak and, when it was finished, the old woman said, "This is not like the kayaks which I used to see."

The man replied, "I do not know how to build any other kind."

Then the boy wished to have a kayak also and so he built one like those he used to see in his own country; but the man was not pleased with it and, fearing that some accident might happen to the boy because the kayak was unsafe, he cut a hole in it, put a large stone in it, and pushed it into deep water, where it sank. Then he built another kayak of the same pattern as his own and gave it to the boy.

When the girl was old enough to marry, the boy took her for his wife. Both families continued to increase, and their descendants still live in the land beyond the sea.

Podluksak

This version is from the South Baffin region.

Podluksak was a murderer. He had stolen the wife of another man. The father and two sons of this man were determined to kill Podluksak. They pursued him, but when Podluksak came to a boat lying on the ground, he hid behind it and stuck out his knife in the path of his pursuers. One of the two sons stumbled, fell on the knife, and was killed. Then Podluksak continued his flight on his sledge. Pursued by the remaining two men, he suddenly jumped from his sledge and buried himself in the snow. When the leading sledge reached him, he moved his whip and caused the dogs to turn away. He then fled to a distant country. When the surviving son reached the place where Podluksak lived, Podluksak shot him with his arrows. Finally, the father arrived to avenge the death of his sons. He saw Podluksak's son playing with a whip and stabbed the boy in his stomach. Podluksak saw what had happened and stabbed and killed the murderer of his son.

Murdering a Stranger

This version is from the South Baffin region.

One day Noodelwa and Ekkomalo were going to move from Ssauniqtung to a camp on the ice. They asked Akygerjew, who was very fleet of foot, to accompany them. After they had gone some distance, their dogs caught a scent and began to run. They soon saw a stranger sitting at the breathing hole of a seal. When the stranger saw the sledge coming, he jumped up and started to run away. The dog team was not very far behind him, and the three men tried to kill the stranger. They shot arrows at him, but they missed him.

The stranger was very fast and soon got out of reach of his pursuers. Then Noodelwa jumped off the sledge and began to run after the stranger. The latter, however, proved to be much faster, and after a short while was far ahead of Noodelwa.

When Noodelwa couldn't catch the stranger he said to Akygerjew, "Jump off the sledge and run after him! If you kill him, we will give you his kayak."

But Akygerjew did not respond.

After a short time they said again, "Try to catch him, and we will give you his kayak."

Then Akygerjew jumped off his sledge and began to run after the stranger. In a very short time he was far ahead of the sledge and began to draw near to the fugitive. When the stranger saw that his pursuer was gaining on him, he threw off his jacket in order to run faster. Nevertheless, Akygerjew came nearer and nearer. Then the stranger turned to one side in order to escape. Akygerjew was within shooting distance and sent an arrow after him. It was a bird arrow with a blunt head, so even if it had hit him it would not have killed him.

The stranger, however, turned back, and shouted, "Stop shooting or I will kill you!"

With this he spanned his bow and aimed an arrow at Akygerjew. Akygerjew, however, being very quick on his feet, easily kept out of range. While the two men were thus trying to catch up with each other, trying to kill each other with arrows, the sledge containing Noodelwa and Ekkomalo came nearer. When the sledge was finally in shooting distance, Noodelwa jumped off and shot the stranger. The arrow struck his leg but did not kill him. The stranger simply pulled it out, broke it in two, and threw it down. Then he turned upon Noodelwa and tried to kill him; but while he was doing so, Ekkomalo shot an arrow which hit his leg. The stranger tried to take it out but was not able to do so.

He cried, "Stop!" and, with this, fell down dead.

Ekkomalo tried to take his arrow out of the stranger's leg but could only remove it by cutting it out. They found the house of the stranger whom they had killed and Akygerjew took possession of his kayak.

This version is from the South Baffin region.

An Agdlaq is a land bear (grizzly bear).

Tale of an Agdlaq

Two men in Tununirn were out caribou hunting. An agdlaq came up from behind and killed one of them. His companion returned to the village and told what had happened. The people did not believe him and thought that he himself might have killed his friend. Finally they all prepared to accompany the man to the spot where his friend had been killed. They prepared their lances and discovered the animal, which did not see them. Then one of the men made a noise like a siksik (ground squirrel) but the agdlaq did not take any notice. They repeated the noise and this time the agdlaq heard them. As soon as it turned upon them, they all lay down on their sides, resting on one elbow. As soon as the bear reached the man who had lost his friend, he arose and walked towards the animal, while the others remained on the ground, crying like ground squirrels in order to distract the bear. The agdlaq attacked the man, who jumped over the animal. Every time it turned on him, he jumped over it, at the same time stabbing it with his lance. Thus he killed it. When the agdlaq was dead, the other people stood up.

The man said to them, "You did not believe me and you thought that I had killed my friend. Why don't you kill me now?"

Then the agdlaq was dragged back to the place where it had first been discovered. The people cut it up and left it there. They found the bones of caribou, ground squirrels, and other animals. They also found the bones of the man whom the agdlaq had killed. The agdlaq had used the man's chest to store caribou fat. The meat that the agdlaq had kept was left in the animal's lair by the people.

This version is from the Kivallik region.

The Emigration of Women

Once two parties went hunting together. For some reason, one party killed the other and went back to stay with the wives of the men they had killed. In time, the women found out that their husbands had been murdered and they planned their revenge. There were two women living in one hut and when one of the murderers was asleep beside one of these women, the other stabbed him with her knife.

Then all of the women made their escape to another part of the country. They had children by the men who had murdered their husbands. Most of the children were boys. Each woman married a son of one of the other women.

One day two men came to the houses in which the women lived. They had been carried off on the ice when sealing and had finally reached the shore.

One of the men entered a hut where there were only two women, while the other one happened to enter a hut in which there were many women. They were so glad to see a man again that they all pounced on him and in the struggle he was smothered to death. The other man fared better but he had to be guarded by the two women he lived with to prevent the others from getting him.

This version is from the North Baffin region (Igloolik-Anne Kappianaq).

The Woman who Escaped to the Moon

It is said that there was a woman who lived in constant fear of her husband, who beat her. One night, when the moon was bright in the sky and the woman was taking a quiet walk, she decided that she would continue walking until the snow was hard enough that she would leave no tracks.

After a while, she reached such snow. She turned her back to the moon and cried out, "Moon, up there! Come and get me. Moon, up there! Come and get me."

Then there was a noise like the pitter-patter of many dogs and a man hissing commands to his dogs, "Pualukittuq, Aqsiq."

There was a crack of a whip with each command to the dogs.

"Get on the qamutiik, but keep your eyes shut. Do not open your eyes," the woman was told. She did as the man said, covering her eyes with her hands.

When they first took off, there were the usual sounds of a dog team, but then there was no more crunching of snow and ice beneath them. The sound of wind was all around, and this struck the woman as strange so she tried to steal a peek by opening one hand. Her mitten immediately flew off.

"There goes my mitten," she cried. The man muttered that she need not worry.

They travelled like that for a long time until the qamutiik landed on ground. The woman knew they had landed when the normal sounds of a dog team running on the snow returned.

Eventually the man said, "Go ahead, open your eyes." She opened her eyes.

She saw brightly lit windows and people outside their houses. The strange thing about the people's attire was that the fur trims around their hoods were gossamer.

As the dog team passed the people, they shouted, "You just pass by, you just pass by, you just pass by!"

As it turned out, these people were the stars in the night sky with their gossamer fur trims.

Then the man told her to again keep her eyes shut, and she did. Again the same thing happened. The crunch of the snow and ice was no longer beneath them. They travelled like that for a long time, until the normal sounds that dog teams make came back. The man told her to open her eyes, and she did. She saw that they had arrived at a camp on the moon and a lit window could be seen. There was seal meat, walrus meat, and caribou meat there, piled on racks. And there were live creatures all around the camp. The man told the woman to enter the dwelling and to seat herself on the bed platform opposite the pantry, where she would sleep.

She saw two neighbours inside, kneeling with their hands between their legs. She was warned not to give in to laughter and to hide her hands inside her amauti once she entered because there was a person about to enter the dwelling who would try to make her laugh by acting silly. If she could not help herself and started to laugh, she was to show her hands through the neck of her amauti and pretend that they were polar bears. She was to blow on her hands.

The woman entered the dwelling. There were two people already seated on the bed platform. They hugged their knees close to their chests and the woman could see that they had no innards.

As they sat on the platform they said, "It is because we snickered that we are this way. It is because we snickered that we are this way."

The woman realized that these people had given in to their laughter, as she had been warned not to do. She sat with them on the bed platform.

A huge pot was brought in from outside the shelter. The pot had inside it human entrails and a huge ulu. Then, in came the owner of the pot and the ulu. This being had short little legs and short little arms, but the clothes on it fit perfectly.

When the being came inside, the old person of the house started to sing a little song: "Here is someone who has just arrived; the one who brought her in placed her on the opposite side of my bed platform."

To which the being replied, "To her shins; to her thighs."

The being told the woman to leave the bed platform and join him as he danced to the song.

"Oh, woe, my forehead. Oh, woe, the scruff of my neck. When the-one-with-a-huge-ulu enters, he cries to her shins; to her thighs," the old person sang.

The being responded with a refrain, "And he with a huge penis," as he danced gleefully.

The woman found this really funny and she started giggling but, as instructed earlier, she pretended her hands were polar bears and she blew on them. She did as she was told and hid her face in her amauti.

"Yech! Your testicles are fatty," she said.

The being went at her, hauling its pot behind it. But it missed disemboweling her, as it could not make her laugh. The woman fled back to the sledge outside the shelter and she and the Man from the Moon made their escape.

The Man from the Moon eventually became the woman's husband and they lived together on the moon.

One day he said to her, "Pick up that shoulder blade by your qulliq and have a look at it."

She picked up the shoulder blade of a seal and she looked through the socket that connected to the ball joint. At first she could not see anything out of the ordinary, for it was dark outside, though the moon was bright. And then in the shoulder blade she saw people playing a game called "amaruujaq." She saw her former husband, her abuser and tormenter, just standing there at the periphery of the activities. He was ragged-looking with his fur trim thin and pauperly. He apparently had suffered greatly since losing his wife. He did not join in on the games. He was cold and ragged with frost on his pathetic fur trim.

From her home on the moon, she would watch and observe the people of her old camp below playing amaruujaq, thus marking the coming of the full moon. She had become pregnant and was expecting a child.

Since her due date was near, her new husband wanted to take her down to Earth and he said, "While your baby breast feeds, do not accept any food caught by your old husband and, likewise, do not use oil rendered from your husband's catch. When you need food, say that you're hungry while you tap on the drying rack and something will drop outside your house. This will be your food. When your qulliq runs out of oil, raise the qulliq and you will see it filled with oil."

Once the woman's new husband had instructed her on how she would receive food and oil, he took her down to the land. She stayed in the old camp and had her baby there. In the old days, it was custom to construct a small igloo for the newborn and its mother where they were left alone. When she was about to give birth, a small igloo was made for her and she gave birth there.

After giving birth, she was bleeding and was spent and hungry, as is normal. As she had been instructed, she started to tap on the drying rack to indicate that she needed food. Soon, she heard a thump just outisde her igloo and she went out to investigate. There was a man holding a haunch of caribou meat for her. She wanted more oil for her qulliq, so she raised the qulliq above her head. Above her, she heard the sound of oil being poured into her qulliq.

Her former husband went out hunting with the other men of the camp and when he came home with a catch he offered food to her. When the woman refused, he was offended and became angry. The woman was just following what she had been told, as she had been warned that both she and the baby would die from eating the cuckold's food.

She told her former husband that she had been warned not to eat from his catch, saying, "I was told if I eat from your catch, my newborn son and I will both die."

The former husband kept on insisting that she eat the offerings of food that he had freshly caught.

"Well, I told you already that we will die if I eat your catch," she replied.

One day, she finally gave in and she ate with her former husband. In the morning, the man went out hunting as usual. When he came back, he went over to his former wife's igloo and saw that she and the baby were still asleep. In actuality, the woman and the baby had both died. Through his great insistence that she eat with him, disregarding the warnings, he had yet again lost the woman who was his wife. Here, the story ends.

Atanaarjuat

This version is from the North Baffin Region.

I n Iksivautaujaak there were two stones that were used as benches by two brothers, Aamarjuaq and Atannaarjuat. The brothers were great hunters. They would harpoon bowhead whales and attach floats made of sealskin, then sit on their stone benches on the shore waiting for their floats to appear on the horizon. When the winds blew from the south, the harpoon floats would become visible out in the sea. With the help of the currents and the wind, the floats ensured that the carcasses of the whales would not be missed as they passed through.

Iksivautaujaak is on Igloolik island.

Aamarjuaq and Atanaarjuat were such successful hunters that the rest of the hunters in their camp were very jealous of their abilities. Each brother had two wives, which made the other men even more envious of the pair. Because the rest of the hunters were jealous of their ability and the fact that they could not outdo the brothers in any way, a plot to kill them was put into motion one spring.

While the brothers were out hunting on the ice not far away from their camp, they could see the other men in the camp preparing for something. When the two brothers returned home they asked two of their wives to go check to see what might be going on with the other men. They told their wives that they had seen some activities silhouetted against the sky while they were out hunting. The women left to investigate, and while they were gone both men went to sleep.

While the wives were with the other hunters they were given instructions to place their long stockings on the side of the tent where their husbands would be sleeping. The women did as they were told. Later that night, while Aamarjuaq and Atanaarjuat slept, the hunters came to their tent, which was marked by the women's stockings. The hunters pounced on the tent, intending to trample the brothers to death.

There was one old woman in the camp who did not wish to see the two brothers killed. She yelled out to the aggressors as if she was warning them: "Atanaarjuap angajuata aqpappaasi!" At that moment, Atanaarjuat sprang to his feet and ran from the tent without any clothing on. Aamarjuaq could not get out of the tent quickly enough. He stood with the tent on his back and struggled to get to the beach. The hunters held on to Aamarjuaq as he walked and stabbed him repeatedly. When he reached the beach, Aamarjauq collapsed and died.

Meanwhile, Atanaarjuat had run out onto the ice without his

"Atanaarjuap angajuata aqpappaasi!" translates as, "Atanaarjuat's's older brother is running for you!"

clothing on. The hunters ran after him, but Atanaarjuat was very fast and he easily lost them. As it was spring, the ground condition easily ate away the flesh on the soles of Atanaarjuat's feet, for he did not have any shoes on. As his feet bled, his footprints were easy to follow. The hunters followed his footprints, eventually coming to a lead that was too wide to cross; that left them no choice but to return to their camp.

At that time there was an old couple staying at Siuraq with their grandchild. They were there to hunt eider ducks and gather eider eggs. Atanaarjuat came to the camp of these two old people with his feet bleeding very badly. The elders saw that his bloody footprints would be very easy for his pursuers to follow, so they cut the soil around his footprints and turned it upside down so that the prints could no longer be seen. They gave him sealskin pants to wear, that belonged to the elderly man, along with a sealskin jacket. There was plenty of seaweed on the beach, as is usually the case in the springtime, so the old couple hid him by covering him with the seaweed.

A short time later, the hunters who were pursuing Atanaarjuat arrived at Siuraq. They immediately questioned the old couple, asking them if they had seen or been visited by a stranger. They replied that they had not seen or heard anything about a visitor recently. The old woman cooked some ducks that they had caught with some dried seaweed, known as Iquuti, for the hunters to eat. It appeared the couple knew nothing of Atanaarjuat, so when they had finished their meal, the hunters decided to return to their camp.

Once they were gone it was safe for Atanarjuat to come out of hiding. He lived with the couple while they looked after his wounds. They used an eider skin to bandage his feet, as the skin contained fat that acted as an ointment to the raw flesh on the soles of his feet. Slowly his wounds healed, and when he was well enough, they all travelled to the mainland, towards Tasiujaq, so they could hunt the plentiful caribou there.

Throughout the spring, Atanaarjuat hunted in order to supply them all with food for the winter months ahead. When the ice melted, he and the old couple's grandson went inland, towards Asiqjuaq, where they made their camp near a lake that was known as a frequent caribou crossing. They stayed in the summer camp at Tasiqjuaq until autumn. Atanaarjuat made himself a warehouse to store some of the caribou that he had caught. They stayed in that location for a long period of time. They even built themselves an Igloo. After they had built their Igloo, Atanaarjuat watered the grounds surrounding the Igloo using the water from the lake, which covered the area with ice, making it extremely slippery. Atanaarjuat had devised a plan to seek revenge on the hunters who had killed his brother and tried to kill him. He decided it was time to find the hunters and set the plan in motion.

First, he went back to the old couple and their family in order to supply them with food provisions, while at the same time moving closer to the area where the hunters camped. He decided to make the trip across to the camp as soon as the strait Ikiq froze over. He had a set of clothes made for his wife who was not involved in the betrayal. For the wife who had betrayed him he packed only skins, from which she would have to make her own clothes.

When the strait had frozen over he started for Igloolik carrying the caribou skins on his back. As he got closer to the camp, the hunters saw him approach. His wife, the one for whom he was carrying clothing, shouted: "Atanaarjuatlu kismi manusinarpajuva," as Atanaarjuat neared the camp. It was still daylight and his wife ran out to meet him. His wife was still wearing the same clothing she had worn all through the summer, so he said to her: "Qangamikiauna taimannaaluk aturtinnakku." He immediately tore her clothing apart and she stood naked in front of him. Then he gave her the clothing that he had brought with him and she got dressed and they went up to the camp together.

Atanaarjuat's other wife, who was involved in the attempt on his life, was now married to someone else. When she saw Atanaarjuat

"Atanaarjuatlu kismi manusinarpajuva" translates as, "Only Atanaarjuat wears mannusinaartuq style parka."

"Qangamikiauna taimannaaluk aturtinnakku" translates as, "I do not know since when I allowed her to wear clothing in this condition."

enter the camp, she too went out to meet him. He also tore her clothing apart, but he left her naked. He gave her the skins that she would be able to make her clothing with and sent her back to her new husband. He had no intentions of taking her back as his wife.

When the hunters returned, they were surprised to find Atanaarjuat in their camp. He invited them all to go with him to his camp so that they might get some meat provisions from his stock. He also told them that he wanted to give them some caribou skins, which they could use as clothing material. The hunters accepted Atanaarjuat's invitation, and Atanaarjuat and his wife left the camp first, in order to arrive home before the rest of the men. As soon as he and his wife arrived at his camp, Atanaarjuat made himself crampons from caribou antlers. The crampons gave him perfect traction against the slippery ground surrounding his Igloo.

After Atanaarjuat and his wife had been in their camp for a while, all the hunters arrived at once, for they were suspicious of Atanaarjuat and knew they needed each other for protection, should he be planning an attack.

Atanaarjuat invited the hunters to a feast and fed them as much as they could eat by bringing more food whenever their plates were nearly empty. When the men could eat no more, he once again went outdoors as he had been doing throughout the feast. But this time, when he returned, he did not carry more food with him. He had on his crampons and a lower section of a caribou antler known as Narruniq, which he used as a club.

He started to club the men with his Narruniq. Many men fled outside to escape Atanaarjuat. The men who fled quickly discovered that the ground outside the igloo was covered in ice. As they fell, Atanaarjuat clubbed each of them to death. He checked for the pulses of the men who were unconscious and if any one of them had a pulse he would club him until his pulse had stopped for good.

When he had killed them all, he returned to their camp where the wives of the hunters now sat helpless without their husbands. Atanaarjuat decided to look after their needs himself. He took care of the women and put their sons to work hunting and working to keep the camp running. Nothing is known of how Atanaarjuat finally died or what happened to him later in his life.

Lice

This version is from Northern Greenland (Polar Inuit).

Once upon a time, there was a woman who had just become a mother and who was horribly tormented by lice on her shoulder.

"It is strange," said she, "that such tiny, toothless animals can bite so hard!"

But, as she stole a glance toward her shoulder, she saw a frightful mouth with great teeth. It was a louse that, angry at what she had said, had assumed the shape of a monster.

The woman was so frightened that she died.

From then on, women who had just given birth were forbidden to mention lice by name, or to complain when they caused irritation.

This happened in the days of our forefathers—in the days when a thoughtless tongue could fashion monsters, which brought about great misfortunes.

Storm Caused by a Loon

This version is from the Kivalliq region.

A long time ago, some men who were at play caught a loon. For sport they pulled out nearly all its feathers, leaving only one long feather in each wing, and let it go. The following winter a great fall of snow set in and, although the people had stores of walrus meat buried under stones, they were unable to reach the meat due to the depth of the snow. Many died of starvation. This storm was caused by the loon in revenge for the ill treatment it had received.

CHAPTER THREE

Journeys and Adventures

Kiviuq is the great traveller of Inuit legend and his adventures dominate this chapter; however, the exploits of Atungait, which resemble those of Kiviuq, are also very interesting. The story of the travelling soul found in this chapter is quite different from the others but clearly relates to the idea of the journey.

The reader may want to be on the lookout for the following:

⊙ *Magic*
⊙ *Violence*
⊙ *Helping spirits*
⊙ *Strange creatures*
⊙ *Cannibals*
⊙ *Revenge*

Kiviuq

This version is from the South Baffin region.

Once upon a time, there was a boy who lived with his grandmother. They were very poor. Since they had no sealskins, the old woman made a shirt from the skins of seagulls for him. One day he was playing with the other children of the village, who made fun of him because of his poverty, and they tore his shirt. He ran home crying, but his grandmother quieted him and mended his shirt. Day after day the boys tore his clothes, until finally the old woman had used up all her thread, and was unable to mend them. She felt very sorry for the boy. She was a great angakkuq, and she was determined to take revenge on the people who mistreated her grandson.

An angakkuq is an Inuit shaman.

She told the boy what to do, then she wrought a spell. The floor of their hut disappeared and in its place was an underground channel leading down to the sea. The boy transformed into a young seal. He swam through the channel and re-appeared in front of the village, in the sea. The people saw the seal and went in pursuit in their kayaks. The young seal swam on and on, luring the people farther and farther away from the land.

Suddenly a gale of wind arose and all the pursuers were lost, except one, whose name was Kiviuq. He had a birdskin amulet in his kayak, which prevented its capsizing.

After a while the gale subsided. Kiviuq was very tired and did not care what became of him. He was sitting idly in his kayak, when suddenly the amulet made a noise. Kiviuq looked up and thought he saw land not far away. He paddled toward it, but soon he saw that what he believed to be land was only the crest of a high wave. Several times he thought he saw land quite near. Finally a low coast appeared and when he came nearer he saw that he had reached a small island. The soil of this island looked red. He went ashore and fell asleep. After he had taken a good rest, he decided to search the island for people.

After travelling for a long time, he came to a place where he saw one hut. Kiviuq went up to it and found an old woman inside. She asked him to enter; and when she saw that his boots were wet, she offered to dry them for him. She invited him to lie down and sleep. Kiviuq looked around in the house and saw a great many severed heads.

One of the heads spoke to him, saying, "The old woman eats all the strangers who enter her house."

Meanwhile, the old woman had gone out and had made a fire

outside. She acted as though she were going to prepare a meal, although Kiviuq did not see any meat in her hut.

Then the head continued to speak, saying, "Take a slab of stone and put it under your jacket, then lie down on your back and sleep."

He obeyed, lay down on his back, and pretended to be asleep. The old woman looked into the house and when she believed her visitor to be asleep, she released her tail from under her jacket. The end of her tail was very sharp. She sharpened her woman's knife and stepped up to the sleeper. She intended to stab him in the heart and in the stomach. She climbed up to the bed, straddled over him, and sat down with full force. She brought her knife down upon his heart and her tail down upon his stomach. But she was not able to do him any harm. She broke her tail on the slab with which he had covered himself.

Then she cried, "Oh, my tail, nin, nin, ne!"

Just then, Kiviuq jumped up and the old woman ran out of the house. Kiviuq tried to take his boots and stockings down from the drying frame, in order to put them on and run away, but as soon as he stretched out his hands, his boots and stockings rose in the air, and when he withdrew his hands they fell down again. He tried several times, but every time he reached out they rose and remained out of reach.

Then he shouted to the old woman and asked her to give him his boots and stockings; but she retorted, "Take them yourself. You see where they are."

Kiviuq replied, "I have been trying to take them, but every time I stretch out my hand they fly up into the air and fall back as soon as I withdraw it."

"Yes," retorted the old woman, "I put them on the drying frame."

When the old woman refused to give them to him, Kiviuq called to his guardian spirit, a bear, to come. As soon as he had called the bear, it was heard growling at a distance. Meanwhile Kiviuq tried again to take down his boots, but every time he tried they rose up into the air. Then he tried to use the fork to take them down, but the fork turned around and pricked him. Then he called again for the bear to come and kill the old woman. The bear was heard much nearer then and the woman grew frightened. She ran into the hut, took down the boots, stockings, and slippers, and gave them to Kiviuq. He put them on and tried to run out of the hut. When he reached the door, it suddenly shut and disappeared. No door was to be seen. When he went back into the interior of the hut, the door appeared again. Again, he tried to rush out. He succeeded in escaping, although the door shut so suddenly that it tore off part of the tail of his jacket.

He ran down to his kayak, but the old woman took hold of its bow and almost overturned it.

Kiviuq shouted, "I shall kill you with my harpoon!"

The old woman retorted, "I shall kill you with my knife!"

Then Kiviuq threw his spear at her, but it only grazed her hair, as she dodged quickly. She let go of the kayak and Kiviuq paddled away as fast as he could.

He travelled on for a long time without seeing anything. Finally he came to a place where he heard a noise on shore, but he did not see any huts.

He heard some one crying, "Help me ashore!"

He landed and looked around. After a long search, he found a mouse in a pool which was surrounded by steep rocks. The mouse was not able to get out. He helped the mouse and then went back to his kayak and paddled away.

He travelled on for a long time without seeing anyone.

One day, he heard someone crying on shore, "Come and take the dirt from my eye!"

He went ashore, pulled up his kayak, and tried to find the person who was crying; but he only saw the arm bone of a seal and noticed that the small hole in the bone was full of dirt. He cleaned it out and went off.

After a long time he saw a hut on shore. He landed and went up to it. In the hut he found an old woman and her daughter. Near the door of the hut he noticed a large piece of driftwood, which was the younger woman's husband. When the wood wished to go sealing, the young woman put it into the water and it went off by itself. After a while it came back, towing seals. The young woman would go down and carry the seals on her shoulders up to the hut. Kiviuq was invited to enter and he soon married the young woman. The piece of driftwood shouted that it was jealous of him; nevertheless, he stayed there as the young woman's husband.

One day, Kiviuq told his wife that he had lost his mittens while sealing and asked her to make a new pair for him. After a few days he said again that he had lost his mittens. He repeated this several times. As a matter of fact, he had not lost them, but only wanted his wife to make him several pairs of new mittens. He intended to return home and wanted to use the new mittens on his return journey, to replace each pair after it had been worn out by paddling.

One day, while Kiviuq was off sealing, the old woman said to her daughter, "There are lice on your head. Let me louse you."

The young woman held her head down, then her mother took a peg (such as is used in drying skins), and drove it into her head through her ear. When the young woman was dead, her mother skinned her and put on her skin. Now she looked just like the young woman.

Soon Kiviuq arrived, bringing a saddle seal in tow. The old woman went down to the beach, intending to take the seal back on her shoulders, but her knees trembled under her. She was not as strong as the young woman. Kiviuq knew at once that it must be the old woman disguised as his wife and went away, never to return.

He travelled a long time in search of his home and finally reached some huts. It was his village. Those who had been children when he went away were now grown up. Kiviuq's wife had taken another husband, but she deserted him and returned to Kiviuq. All his children had grown up. His oldest son was a good hunter, and was now in command of a whaling boat.

Kiviuq

This version is from the North Baffin region (Igloolik-Anne Kappianaq).

When Kiviuq and his older brother were both young adults, there was an orphan who lived with his grandmother amongst the other villagers. The grandmother lacked clothing materials for her orphan grandson, so she did her best to make clothing out of the skin of ducks and other leftovers. But the villagers often played ball and whenever the orphan got into the ball game, they would tear up the boy's clothing. Kiviuq and his older brother never took part in the roughness toward the orphan. During the ball games, they treated the orphan the same way they treated the other players.

The boy's grandmother felt sorry that the men were tearing up his clothing and bullying him. She was thankful to Kiviuq and his brother for being kind and providing the orphan with clothing materials when the others destroyed his clothes.

One day, when the men went out to sea for a hunt, the grandmother told her grandson to go out and look for a seal pup head at the abandoned camp sites. When the orphan found what he had been asked to find, he brought it back to his grandmother. She softened the seal skin from the head to make a mask. She also filled up a sealskin bucket with water. Into the bucket she submerged her grandson again and again until he was able to hold his breath and had learned how to stay underwater for long periods of time.

One morning, the grandmother took her grandson down to the beach with the seal pup mask.

She told him to swim way out into the sea, raise his left arm and yell, "Where's my sky?"

She let him swim away and as he did he was submerged, just like a seal.

When he resurfaced, she yelled to the men, "Look, there, a seal pup down by the beach!"

When the men saw the seal pup, they rushed to their qajaqs and took off. Earlier, the grandmother had instructed the orphan to resurface from time to time in places where it would be difficult to throw a harpoon. He did this and led the men far into the sea. The men followed the seal pup far, finding it very difficult to catch.

When the orphan was quite a distance from shore, as advised by his grandmother, he resurfaced and yelled, "Where's my sky ugaa, where's my sky ugaa." Then a strong wind came up suddenly. The wind was so strong that most of the men capsized and were lost. The little boy swam back home, having done what he had been told to do.

Ugaa is the sound of a baby seal.

Meanwhile, Kiviuq and his older brother had stayed upright and kept on paddling through the very rough sea. Kiviuq helped his brother stay afloat for some time, but eventually his brother lost his grip and capsized and drowned, leaving Kiviuq alone on the sea. All alone, Kiviuq drifted far into the distance. Strangely, he constantly heard a phalarope singing; the sound seemed to be coming from his qajaq. He drifted like that for days.

He started urinating into his qajaq and whenever he did so, he would say, "Oh, once again I have peed." Whenever he saw a line in the distance as thin as a sealskin rope, he said, "Far away, in the distance, land. Down below, the bottom of the sea. Now they've disappeared." Shortly after, he realized that it was only waves which resembled far-away land. Yet, again and again, he saw a line as thin as a sealskin rope and he said, "Far away, in the distance, land. Down below, the bottom of the sea. And, now they've disappeared."

Again, he saw a thin line that appeared almost red. He said, "Far-away land, not disappearing, far-away land, shallower waters, and it's not disappearing," constantly repeating the words.

When Kiviuq neared the land, which was then unmistakable, he became very tired, as he had been awake for days and days. When he finally got onto the dry land, he tipped his qajaq over and emptied it, as it was full of his urine. Then he lay down and fell asleep instantly.

Much later, he was awakened and heard someone say, "Go get some sleep next door."

But when he awoke he found no one there. Once again, he fell asleep instantly. Time after time, he was awakened and told to go next door but each time he awoke to find no one there.

Later, when Kiviuq was better rested and more aware of his surroundings, he remained lying down and pretended to sleep. Once again, the invisible person tried to wake him, but this time Kiviuq got up suddenly. The invisible person was caught and she immediately started to treat Kiviuq very nicely. She invited him into the sod house to dry off his clothing and told him to get more sleep.

When Kiviuq entered her house, she took his kamiks and inner socks and put them on the drying rack. Then she worked on starting a fire down on the porch. While she was gone, Kiviuq noticed several skulls by the entrance of the house. One of the skulls whispered to him, "You will end up like me, get out! You will end up like me, get out!"

After this warning, Kiviuq immediately tried to take his kamiks from the drying rack, but when he reached for them the drying rack rose up. Time after time, the drying rack did the same thing, preventing him from taking his belongings.

He yelled at the woman who was starting up the cooking fire, "Come in and get my belongings. The drying rack keeps rising up, preventing me from taking them."

The woman replied, "I did my share of putting them on the rack for you, now it's your turn to take them off yourself."

Again, Kiviuq replied, "The drying rack rises up whenever I try to take my belongings. Come in and pick them up for me."

Once again, the woman replied, "I put them on the drying rack for you, now it's your turn to take them down."

Suddenly, a spear magically appeared from the woman's sleeping mat. She was trying to spear Kiviuq!

Kiviuq became very scared and yelled at the woman, "Come in and get my kamiks!"

The woman only repeated, "I put them on the rack for you, now it's your turn to take them down."

Kiviuq then yelled, calling to his polar bear spirit, "Polar bear spirit, come and fetch her!"

And then, above the woman came a loud roar and, once again, Kiviuq yelled to the woman, "Come in and get my kamiks for me!" But the woman only repeated her reply.

So, Kiviuq called upon his polar bear spirit again, louder this time, yelling, "Polar bear spirit, come and fetch her!"

Suddenly, a polar bear roared from very nearby. This time, the woman fell down on the ground, face first. She was panicked and she yelled very rapidly, "Sealskin kamiks, outer socks, inner socks!" She was handing back Kiviuq's kamiks, inner socks, and all the rest to him. But, when Kiviuq tried to exit the sod house, the doorway closed in on him and he barely escaped. The door closed so quickly part of his caribou parka was torn off and left behind.

He ran down to his qajaq and took off. The woman followed him toward the beach with her ulu in her hand, saying, "I would have struck you with this!"

She pretended to strike Kiviuq with her ulu and Kiviuq almost capsized from the force of it. In return, Kiviuq pretended to strike the woman with his oar, even though she was some distance away.

He yelled, "I would have harpooned you with this!"

The woman fell backward, landing on her buttocks. Her ulu smashed when she fell and turned into thin ice across the water where Kiviuq was paddling. The ice stopped him on the spot. But he pretended to strike the thin ice with his oar and that caused a path to open so that he could continue paddling.

After paddling for some time, he was no longer paddling through ice. Then the paddling became difficult again. He had difficulty moving forward.

From the land, he could hear someone yelling constantly, "Come over and lift me up. Come over and lift me up."

So, Kiviuq landed and he looked around. The only thing he could see was a lemming trying to climb a small hill, so he lifted it up. After that, he had no difficulty paddling forward in the water.

Again, he paddled for some time until, once again, he heard someone yelling from the land, "Come over here and take this dirt out of my eye. Come over here and take this dirt out of my eye."

Once again, he began to have difficulty paddling forward. So, he landed and looked around. He could not see anything that would have dirt in its eye. The only thing he found was a seal bone. He removed some moss from a hole in the seal bone and then climbed back into his qajaq. After that, he was able to continue paddling forward.

After paddling for quite a while, Kiviuq saw a qarmaq. He landed and went over to it. He looked inside and saw a woman working on a sealskin.

She said, "Is there a hairy one nearby?"

When she looked up, her eyelids hung loose. She was not able to see. She turned her head down again, tending to her sealskin.

Kiviuq then spit inside the qarmaq and the woman said, "What does not drip, did drip today?"

This time, when she looked up, she cut a piece of her eyelid off and ate it. Kiviuq realized she was not human and he quickly got into his qajaq and departed.

He paddled for quite awhile and then he encountered some other people; women decorated with beads. He ended up living with the women for some time, but then he took their beads and left the women behind in their camp.

Then, after travelling a while longer, Kiviuq reached the camp of a mother and daughter who lived alone. The daughter was very strong. Kiviuq lived with the women and eventually made the daughter his wife. Whenever Kiviuq caught a bearded seal or a ringed seal, he usually dragged the mammal behind his qajaq. When he got back to the camp, his wife carried the mammal back from the beach to higher ground without any trouble.

After being married to that strong woman for a while, Kiviuq started to notice that a tree trunk that lay between he and his wife as they slept sometimes made crackling sounds. He also noticed that whenever the tree trunk was pushed out to the sea, it returned to the camp with a bearded seal or ringed seal, which it had caught. The tree trunk was placed between Kiviuq and his wife during the night and whatever the tree trunk had caught that day was placed between the tents.

When Kiviuq was out hunting, he brought back what he had caught and the tree trunk did the same. Kiviuq became suspicious and asked his wife why the tree trunk made crackling sounds. His wife, assuming her mother was asleep, whispered to Kiviuq that the tree trunk was her mother's husband. However, her mother had not been asleep.

Her mother said, "He's the husband of both of us."

Kiviuq and the tree trunk did some hunting together. When they came back from hunting, Kiviuq's wife went down to the beach to collect what Kiviuq had caught. But when she tried to lift the seal as she had done so many times before, she dropped it. She tried again but she was unable to carry the seal on her back. Kiviuq asked her why she was unable to carry the seal and she replied that nothing was wrong. But when she started to walk, Kiviuq noticed that some of her skin was falling off and that her skin looked too large for her body.

When Kiviuq noticed that his strong wife had suddenly become very weak and that her skin appeared too large for her body, he knew that the weak, frail old woman must have killed his wife and put on her skin to trick him. As soon as he realized what the old woman had done, he left the camp and never returned.

He travelled for a long while and autumn became winter. He came upon two young men who were hunting seals at the floe edge. One of the young men told him a story. He said that when he and his brother were children, they lost their father. He told Kiviuq that many men had capsized and lost their lives during a fierce storm. The young man mentioned that his father's name was Kiviuq. When the man finished his story, Kiviuq told them his name and that he was in fact their father. They all became very happy and started getting ready to return to their village.

The two young men had been reconnected with their father, whom they had lost when they were very young. On their way home, Kiviuq asked if their mother was still alive. His sons said that she was alive and that she had remarried.

When they were close enough to be heard from the village, Kiviuq yelled, "Aasiggaat, Aasiggaat!" His wife was outside and she heard Kiviuq's unmistakable voice.

She yelled back, "Only my husband calls out 'Aasiggaat' when he approaches the village! Aasiggaat, aasiggaasiggaasiggaat!"

She was so thankful that she kept saying, "Only my husband would call out 'Aasiggaat' to announce his arrival. Only Kiviuq would call out 'Aasiggaat!' Aasiggaat, aasiggassiggassiggat!"

When Kiviuq reached the village, he saw that his former wife had aged. She looked different and she had remarried. He had no intention of hurting her new husband, but her new husband left the tent and never returned. It turned out that he had thought Kiviuq intended to kill him, assuming that Kiviuq was not human and had returned to take his life. So, he ran out and decided never to return, although Kiviuq had never intended to kill him.

Atungait

This version is from the North Baffin region (Igloolik-Harvay Paniaq).

It is said that Atungait lived with his siblings and other people in a camp when he decided that he would attempt to circumnavigate Qikiqtaaluk (Baffin Island).

So, he started preparing for the trip. He directed the women of the camp to scrape bearded seal hides to vie for the privilege of going with him on the trip. The women were so intent on the task that some of them injured their wrists. On it went until only two women were left.

The younger of the two women broke her wrist and so the older one was chosen to go with him. The scraping contest, it turned out, was to help him choose a wife. After choosing a wife this way, he was ready to embark on his journey to circumnavigate the island.

On their journey, Atungait and his wife first came upon a camp of cannibals. If someone cut him or herself in the camp of cannibals, the rest of the camp would eat that person.

They were not long in the camp when someone said, "One of us has not been seen for a while now; perhaps he's been eaten."

And someone else replied, "Perhaps it was he whom I saw mounted on a big monstrous brown dog" (referring to the helper spirit of the man in question).

Yet another replied, "Yes. Could have been him, could have been him. Perhaps it was Nukkakittaq who ate him."

In this camp where people who cut themselves were eaten, two little girls were picking some flesh off a recently eaten human corpse when the older of the two cut herself. She begged her sister not to say anything about her cut.

But the younger girl blurted out, "My sister just cut herself."

When the rest of the cannibals heard this, they ate the older girl. She would not have been eaten if her sister had not said anything.

Atungait and his wife left the cannibals and continued on their journey. When they came upon another camp, they were taken in as guests and, perhaps because of custom, they were assigned the middle section of the bed platform between their hosts.

A little girl entered the place where Atungait and his wife were staying and, just as quickly, she left. As it turned out, her grandmother had asked her to check the tray on the floor for any drippings from a recent meal.

The pelvis usually refers to a small serving of tender seal meat offered as a sign of respect to someone not of one's household, but this reference implies something sinister.

Soon, the little girl returned, carrying an ice pick and mat. Upon entering the house, she said, "I'm here to take your guests' helping of the pelvis."

Then she said, "My grandma is making a mash of human and wolf brains. She wants me not to say anything so I'm not saying anything."

As it turned out, the old woman was concocting something with which to poison Atungait, exactly as the little girl had blurted out.

The little girl left again and, soon after, came back for the third time. She announced, "The guest is invited to come and try the mash."

So, Atungait went to taste the old woman's mash. After he entered her house, he ate the proffered mash hungrily, even licking the serving tray. After he was done eating, he placed the tray, which was made from a shoulder blade, between his legs and turned it over before engaging himself in conversation with the old woman.

They talked at length before the old woman turned the tray over and offered him some more mash "Now, please have some more mash," she said.

So, Atungait again ate the food hungrily and, as before, licked the tray when it was gone. When he was done he turned the tray over and placed it between his legs.

They talked some more and Atungait would once in a while turn over the tray, but it was still empty. He would turn the tray over and over again as they talked, but it remained empty.

It was now late in the night. They all went to bed and slept. In the morning, the old woman who had prepared the poison to kill Atungait was found dead from her own mash.

After a time, Atungait and his wife were again on their way. They travelled along the shoreline in their boat but slowly the shoreline became rougher until they found themselves gliding along the bottom of a cliff. Soon there was no more beach on which to land, but Atungait did not want to backtrack, having already worked so hard to get to this point.

He got closer to the wall of the cliff to see if they could climb out. They could, so he told his wife to keep her eyes shut as they climbed the rock face. Atungait called on his dogs to follow them, "H'ai Atungait. H'ai Atungait."

The dogs followed their master as he climbed up the cliff, but Atungait's favourite dog could not climb out with the rest for it was too old. The dog was lifted up on a rope, but it slipped out of the rope and fell. Then Atungait's wife opened her eyes briefly. She got disoriented and dropped one of her mittens but she did not fall.

Having safely made it to the top of the cliff, they continued their

The Inuktitut phrase for "is he the raven" ends like the crowing of a raven.

journey on land. They were headed in the general direction of the shoreline when they happened upon another camp.

They stayed in the camp as the days got longer. It was a beautiful day and Atungait was feeding his dogs. He could see the people of the camp playing ball down on the ice. Then Atungait noticed that two old women had come over to his side of the camp. He just looked at them awhile and then he remarked, "These two are like ravens."

The two old women replied, "Is he the raven? Is he the raven?" as they pecked about on the ground where Atungait had chopped up some meat.

They continued to peck on the ground and then one of them circled Atungait. He cracked his whip at her and said, "Ravens don't come any closer than that."

Night came and Atungait and his wife went to bed and slept. The old woman that Atungait had shooed away with his whip appeared from the vaporous fog just above the floor in a qajaq. She glided up to the edge of the bed platform, over the bed, and poised herself right above Atungait's toes. She held a harpoon in her hand. Then, just as she was ready to harpoon Atungait, he wiggled his big toes and the apparition disappeared. In the morning, when they woke up, Atungait and his wife learned that the old woman had died during the night.

Soon after, Atungait and his wife were again on their way. They again came upon a camp where the people were playing a game of ajagaq with a rabbit skull and Atungait joined in. The people of the camp were tiny and only came up to Atungait's chest, but their equipment, such as their qamutiiks, was perfectly proportional to normal-sized people.

Atungait spent days in the camp, joining in on the games, because he liked the rabbit-head toy. The pin they used for the game was made of copper and at the other end of the string was a bob made from cartilage. This Atungait liked.

Eventually, Atungait began to plan to leave the camp. One night, he claimed to have diarrhea and was constantly going outside to relieve himself, climbing back into bed when he returned. In actuality, he was going outside to cut the lashings on the qamutiiks because he was plotting to steal the rabbit head from the ajagaq game.

When morning came, Atungait and his wife got up and started to pack up their belongings to again take up their journey. They were ready, with the wife already on the qamutiik, when Atungait said that he wanted to join in on the game for a bit.

During the game his wife went over to ask him to get going, as they were ready to leave. He was about to go when he told his wife to just wait a moment. When it was Atungait's turn in the game, he grabbed the rabbit head and ran outside. As soon as he was outside, he left with everything that he owned.

The people he stole from were heard shouting, "Where is our rabbit head? Give us back our rabbit head!" But they could not walk very quickly because of their small legs and Atungait got away easily.

The people quickly prepared their qamutiiks to pursue the thief and some of them actually left, but their qamutiiks collapsed as they got to the shoreline. All the lashings on their qamutiiks had been cut by Atungait the night before.

But Atungait had missed one and that qamutiik took on the chase, its owner shouting after Atungait, "Give us back our rabbit head!"

The pursuers were gaining on Atungait, so he took out his arrows and drew his bow. He shot his arrows right in front of the lead dog to make it turn and veer off. The dog veered away so suddenly from Atungait's arrows that the qamutiik tipped over and its occupants tipped over with it.

So, Atungait's hapless pursuers could not catch him and he got away. Atungait and his wife continued on their journey to circumnavigate Qikiqtaaluk. Here the story ends.

The Soul

This version is from the Kivalliq region.

Once upon a time, an old woman who had died was buried and then a raven came and began to eat her. Her soul entered the body of the raven and she became a raven. The raven laid eggs, but soon after a man came and shot the bird, took it into his house, and gave it to a dog to eat.

Then the woman's soul entered the dog. When the dog was struck by people, it pretended to be sick and cried, "Ma, ma, ma!"

The dog had pups. After some time a wolf came and killed the dog and ate it. Then the woman's soul was in the wolf and the wolf had pups. The wolf was very hungry, but could not run fast. When it followed the pack and came to the place where they had killed a caribou, it found that the other wolves had eaten all the meat and had left nothing but the bones.

The wolf asked, "Why can't I keep up with you?"

And an old wolf told it, "You ought to spread your claws when you run and not keep them closed."

The wolf did so, and when they ran again it ran so fast that the others were left behind. It killed a caribou and ate all it wanted, while the other wolves came later on.

The wolf was eventually caught in a trap set by hunters and was killed.

Then the woman's soul became a caribou and the caribou had young ones. Soon, winter set in and the ground was frozen and covered with snow.

The caribou said to the others, "Why can I not find anything to eat?" And the others told it to scratch away the snow with its forefeet and it would find moss underneath. The caribou did not like its companions and went off in the direction of a village, where it was seen and killed by a man.

Then the soul went into a walrus and the walrus had young ones. This walrus became hungry and went down to the bottom of the sea to dig clams, but the clams would not open their shells and it came up still hungry.

It said to the other walruses, "I cannot get anything to eat. The clams refuse to open their shells for me."

Then the other walruses said, "When you go to the bottom of the sea, say, 'Eok, eok, eok!'"

It did so and as soon as it said, "Eok!" the clams opened their shells and it had all it wanted to eat. Soon after this the walrus was caught by a man and the soul of the woman went into a ground seal, which had young ones. The ground seal was also taken by a hunter. Then the soul went into a seal, which had young ones.

This seal met another seal, and the other seal said, "There are two men waiting for seals at holes in the ice. You go to that hole, I will go to this one."

But the seal in which the woman's soul was embodied said, "No, when that hunter was a boy, he was lazy. He would not put snow into his mother's kettle. He does not deserve to have good luck."

The other seal went to his hole and the hunter pierced it with his harpoon, but only wounded it.

The wounded seal cried out, "You have hurt me, and your harpoon is cold." The two seals got together and the seal with the woman's soul inside it told the other seal to go to the hole of the hunter who had been lazy as a child. The seal refused to go to the hole because he did not want to bring luck to such a person. Then the seal in which the soul was embodied went to the good hunter, who killed it and took it home.

When they arrived at the house, the seal stayed close to the harpoon and said, "Why does the woman not come and take the harpoon into the house?"

Soon the hunter's wife came and took the harpoon, and then the soul went into her.

After some time she had a child, who was no other than the old woman. When she came to be about eight or ten years of age, she would go out to see what game the hunters brought in, and she recognized her old companions. She knew them by the name each was called by his own kind. When she grew older, she told the other people in what animals her soul had been, and what the animals liked and disliked. She told them that while she was a walrus, other walruses used to come up and kiss her until her nose became sore. She also told them that the ground seals were very good, but that they always looked very angry. She said that when she was a seal, she used to play all the time, but that as a wolf she was hungry.

On account of this tale it is customary to bring in the harpoon line at once after the seal has been taken into the house.

The Soul that Let itself Be Born Again in all the Animals of the Earth

This version is from the Netsilik region.

There was once a great shaman who wanted to see what it was like to live the life of all animals. So, he let himself be reborn in all kinds of animals. For a time he was a bear. That was a tiring life; bears were always walking, even in the dark they roamed about, always on the wander.

Then he became a fjord seal; the seals were always in the humour for playing. They were ever full of merry jests and they leaped about among the waves, frolicsome and agile, till the sea began to move. Their high spirits set the sea in motion.

At that time there was not much difference between humans and seals, for the seals could suddenly turn themselves into human shape. When in human form they were skilful with the bow and amused themselves by setting up targets to shoot at, targets of snow, just as men make them.

Once the shaman was a wolf, but then he almost starved to death until one of the wolves took compassion on him and said, "Get a good hold of the ground with your claws and try to keep up with us when we run." He did this from then on and so he learned to run and catch caribou.

Then he turned into a muskox, and it was warm in the middle of the big herds, he said.

Afterward he became a caribou. They were strangely restless animals, always timid; in the middle of their sleep they would spring up and gallop away. They became scared at nothing and so there was no fun in being a caribou.

In this way the shaman lived the life of all animals. This took place in times long ago, when animals often were humans. People believe that there was a time when there was not much difference between an animal's soul and a human's soul. All living things were very much alike.

Hardships and Famine

Traditional life was predictably difficult and uncertain. Survival depended on the skills, fortitude, and knowledge of the hunters. Stories of hardship, particularly famine, are very common and this chapter gives a clear sense of the horrors of starvation.

The reader may want to be on the lookout for the following:

- *The fear of cannibalism*
- *Violence*
- *Community action*
- *Starvation*
- *Natural disaster*
- *Magic*
- *Transformation*

Ijimagasukdjukdjuaq

This version is from the South Baffin region.

Ijimagasukdjukdjuaq and his wife lived in a large village. He was a cannibal. He used to ask his wife to go out and gather heather. When she came back he would tell her to cook human flesh for him because he had killed a person while she was gone. The woman never ate human flesh. He had killed a great many people, and finally only his wife and he himself remained in the village. Then he resolved to kill her.

One day he sent her out to gather heather. The woman, however, was afraid of her husband, and resolved to flee from him. She filled her jacket, her boots, and her trousers with heather and arranged the stuffed garments to look like a person sitting on the ground. She told the garments to call out if her husband stabbed them. Then she wished for snow to fall. She had hardly made the wish when snow began to fall, and continued until it was so deep that it entirely covered her.

In the evening, Ijimagasukdjukdjuaq went out to look for his wife. He found her clothing, filled with heather, sitting on the ground, and he believed it to be his wife. He tried to kill her with his knife and the figure cried out as though it felt the pain. Soon, however, he discovered his mistake. He thought that his wife must be nearby, and probed the snow all around with his knife. But he did not find her. Then he returned to his hut. As soon as he left the spot where she hid, she came forth from under the snow, shook the heather out of her clothing, and put it on again. Then she ran away.

After a time, she saw a piece of ice set up as a fox trap. She went inside to rest and to wait until the man to whom the trap belonged came back to check on it. Some time afterward, she heard steps; a man arrived, and she soon realized it was her brother. They went together to his home, where there were quite a number of huts, and she stayed there. After some time, Ijimagasukdjukdjuaq went in pursuit of his wife.

The people cried, "Ijimagasukdjukdjuaq the cannibal is coming!"

Ijimagasukdjukdjuaq replied, "Who told you so?"

They shouted back, "The woman who passed here in a boat told us so."

They did not tell him that his wife was staying with them.

In the evening, the people went into the dancing house and invited him to join them. In the dancing house they had two supports put up and a tightrope stretched across.

Ijimagasukdjukdjuaq's brother-in-law said to his friends, "Bring in my harpoon. I want to go caribou hunting tomorrow."

Meanwhile, the other people were swinging on the tightrope. They had their hands tied to a stick by which they hung across the rope while others laughed to see them swinging. Finally Ijimagasukdjukdjuaq's turn came, and while he was hanging from the tightrope, his brother-in-law killed him with his harpoon.

Igimagajug, the Cannibal

This version is from the Kivalliq region.

Igimagajug was hunting seals one day. He caught a ground seal and brought it to his hut. While he was away, Igimagajug's wife had given birth to a still-born child. When he reached the door of his hut, he called to her to come out and haul the seal in. She replied that it would be better for her to remain in the hut, telling him what had happened, but he only became angry. He commanded her to come and haul the seal inside.

This offended Nuliajuk, the mother of the sea mammals, who withheld seals from the people of the village. As a result, the villagers bcame very hungry.

Because there were no seals to eat, Igimagajug killed his father-in-law and his mother-in-law and ate them. He killed all the other people nearby, and also ate them. His wife became afraid that he might want to eat her also, so one day when he was away sealing, she prepared to escape. She was a powerful angakkuq. She made a figure by filling her clothing with moss. She told it to turn its back toward the door when

An angakkuq is an Inuit shaman.

Igimagajug entered and to cry, "Uk, uk!" if Igimagajug stabbed it with his knife. Then she built a small snow house nearby and made a peephole in one wall.

Soon Igimagajug came back from hunting. The figure turned its back upon him and he stabbed it. Then it cried out, "Uk, uk!" When Igimagajug discovered that the figure was nothing but clothing filled with moss, he sat down, angry. He was very hungry, so he cut a piece out of his leg and ate it.

The wound hurt him and he said, "I did not think it hurt other people when I killed and ate them, but I find it hurts me."

Igimagajug wished to know whether his wife had gone far, so he wrought a spell by pulling upon a seal line. When he asked the line a question and the answer was in the affirmative, the line would become heavier; if the answer was in the negative, the line would become lighter.

He asked, "Is my wife nearby?" The line became a little heavier.

"Is she close by?" The line became very heavy.

He then took his spear and went out and probed the snow to find her. Once, he struck the small snow house that she had built and his spear passed between her fingers, but still he did not find her.

On the following day, Igimagajug went sealing and, while he was gone, his wife started for the village where her brother lived. When Igimagajug came back from sealing, he saw her tracks and started in pursuit. When she saw him coming, she hid behind some hummocks of rough ice. When he came to the place where her tracks stopped, he kicked the snow away, but could not find her.

In the meantime, she continued to run toward her brother's house. When she reached the house, she told her brother and his friends what had happened.

The following day, Igimagajug started out in search of his wife and arrived at the village. He found the men at play, swinging on a tightrope with a line tied around each wrist. He joined the game and tried it once. Then he took a rest and the other men had their hands tied; each swung in his turn. Finally Igimagajug's turn came again. The line was tied around his wrists.

While Igimagajug held his hands up, his brother-in-law, who up to this time had pretended to be very friendly, said, "You killed and ate my father, my mother, and the other people!"

Igimagajug questioned, "Who said so?"

"Your wife."

"What is my wife's name?"

"Pubelarleyark," replied her brother.

"I don't see her," said Igimagajug.

He had hardly said so when his wife stepped forth from her hiding place.

When he saw her, he said, "You ate your father's and your mother's hands and feet!"

But she replied, "No! I took them out of the kettle. I only pretended to eat them and I cried very much to lose my father and my mother."

When she said that, the other people rushed upon Igimagajug and killed him with their spears.

Karnapik, the Cannibal

This version is from the South Baffin region.

Unikkaaqtuat

One winter, the people at Anarnitung were starving. Karnapik's daughter was dying and he had given up all hope of her recovery. He asked his wife to give him a piece of rope so that he could tie his daughter up in a blanket. He intended to take her out of the house through the porch and let her die outside. His wife, however, asked him to wait and keep her a little longer. After some time, the daughter died. Her parents were so hungry that they contemplated eating their daughter's body. They resisted the urge for some time, but eventually they gave in and ate their daughter's flesh. This kept Karnapik and his wife alive for some time, but when they had eaten the body entirely they knew they would soon be hungry again.

So, Karnapik took his daughter's thigh bone and used it as a speaking trumpet to call the people.

He stepped in front of the door of his house and shouted through the bone, "Kill someone!"

Then the people killed one of their neighbours and all ate of his flesh.

When they had finished, he again stepped in front of his house and shouted through his trumpet, "Kill another one!"

This time they killed more than one person and again they all ate of the flesh. When they had finished, they became hungry again.

Karnapik again used his dreadful trumpet and shouted, "Kill another one!"

By now they had killed quite a number and only a few people were left. They boiled the human flesh in Karnapik's house and when it was done he invited the survivors to come and partake of it.

When all the flesh was gone and the people became hungry, Karnapik again blew his trumpet, and shouted, "Kill another one!"

Thus their number became less every day.

Karnapik's wife boiled the flesh and invited the people to come and partake of it. After a few meals it was all gone. Finally, only two villagers were left.

When Karnapik shouted through his trumpet, "Kill another one!" one of these killed the other one and Karnapik's wife boiled the flesh.

When all of this flesh was gone, Karnapik stepped out of the house. This time he did not shout through his trumpet, but went and killed the last survivor, whom he and his wife ate.

About this time, two strangers, who were roaming about the

country, came to Karnapik's house. One of them looked in at the window and saw Karnapik eating human flesh.

Karnapik saw him, and said, "We are no longer human beings. We have become supernatural beings."

They told the strangers how they had killed all the people in the village and how they had used the speaking trumpet made of the thigh bone of their dead girl. The visitors, after hearing what had happened, left at once. Karnapik and his wife stayed behind, not daring to join human beings again, since they knew they had become supernatural beings.

Both of them probably died through want of flesh.

Separated from Camp

This version is from the South Baffin region.

There was a camp near Qivitung on the floe ice, some distance from the land. The people had been living there for some time, when all of a sudden a heavy swell came and broke up the ice under the houses, compelling the inhabitants to make their way to the land the best they could.

In one of the houses lived an old man. The ice broke right under his house and split it in two, leaving the old man in one half of the house. He refused to join the people in their escape and stayed where he was. His son, with whom he was living, had a wife and three children. The youngest child was still in its mother's hood. As the ice broke, the mother took the baby out of her hood and placed it in the hood of her oldest child. She left the child and the baby with their grandfather and fled from the camp with the rest of the people. While trying to reach the shore, some of the people fell between the cracks of the ice and many of them drowned. The son of the old man led the way out. The women had not had time to take any of their belongings except their knives and needle cases. The men had only their spears, knives, and harpoon lines. After five days of dangerous travelling, they reached the shore. They had no food and no water to drink.

Once they reached land, they searched for a pond. They discovered one, but after they cut through the ice, the water was found to be salt, although the pond was quite a distance from the shore. After some time they found another pond, which had fresh water. Then they began to drink. Another group of people who had fled the camp on the ice came ashore and discovered the first group of travellers.

When they saw the others drinking, they shouted, "Don't drink all the water! Leave some for us!"

But the pond was so large that there was plenty for all of them. Some of them had drunk too much water, and complained of feeling cold. Others, who had not taken so much, said that they felt warm and comfortable after drinking. Those who had taken too much water died before they reached their destination, the old camp onshore where they had lived before moving to the floe ice. Only a very few of the people who had left the village survived to sing their old songs.

Kating Saved his Family in Time of Famine

This version is from the South Baffin region.

At Isortuqdjuaq, in Kingawa, the people had been hunting caribou. In the fall, when they were preparing to move camp, the frost set in very suddenly, covering the sea with ice. Heavy snows fell and the people were unable to leave. Soon they were starving. Many people died; but in one house an old woman named Quawallow, her three sons, and her daughter, survived. The name of her eldest son was Kating. Kating decided to go to Niutang to ask for help from the people who lived there. He left his dog with his mother, so that they might eat it after he was gone.

A short time after Kating left, his mother couldn't find the dog. She went in search of it and found that its footprints led to a neighbouring hut. She had thought that the people inside the hut were dead; however, when she went in, she found them still alive.

She asked, "Is my dog in here?"

The woman in the house denied that it was there, saying she had not seen it. Quawallow insisted, saying that she had seen its tracks leading in. She searched for her dog and finally, when she lifted the heather, found its skinned body.

She became very angry and took it home. There she told her children that the neighbour woman had killed her dog with the intention of eating it. Quawallow knew that her son would have to walk a long way before he would be able to return and that her family needed meat to survive. Soon the neighbours were all dead and Quawallow and her children were living on the meat of her dog.

Kating, on reaching Niutang, found that the people there had caught two whales in the fall of the preceding year. He told them how the people in Isortuqdjuaq were starving. He told them that a few had tried to reach other places, but that they may have died in the attempt, since nothing had been heard from them. The people of Niutang were very kind to Kating and after a while he forgot his starving mother, his brothers, and his sisters. After a few days he was ready to return. The people gave him a whale bone toboggan and an old dog. They loaded the toboggan with whale meat, whale skin, and blubber.

When he was ready to start, they said to him, "Stay here. Your mother is probably dead by now."

But Kating replied, "No, I think she is alive."

Then he started on his way to Kingawa.

When he reached Kingawa, he went to the window of his mother's hut and asked, "Are you all dead?"

His mother replied, "No, there is life in us yet."

Then Kating went in and gave them the whale meat and whale skin, and his mother told him what had happened while he was away.

They continued to live in Kingawa. Kating's brothers, sisters, and mother became ill, so Kating went out sealing in order to strengthen them with the meat he would catch. He found a seal hole and went back home. He was afraid the seal might have heard him and would not return for a long time, so he stayed at home for two days. On the third day he went to the seal hole and waited for the seal to come. On the following morning the seal came and he harpooned it, cut it up, and took it home. When his brothers and sisters saw it, they thought it was delightful, and they started a fire and cooked the meat. Then they felt better and Kating took the rest of the meat home.

Kating's mother did not feel very well. She wished to have a ptarmigan. Kating succeeded in killing one. Then she felt better, but soon afterward she grew worse again. Then she wished for a piece of caribou meat. Kating went hunting and succeeded in killing a caribou. He took part of the meat home and his family was very much delighted. They ate it and his mother felt quite well again.

By then spring had come and the seals were basking on the ice. He was able to kill enough seals so that they were no longer in need.

Taboos and Starvation

Unikkaaqtuat

Once upon a time, two boats started from Netchillik down Koukdjuaq and travelled northward along the shore of Fox Channel. One of the boats returned the same summer. The men in that boat had taken some walrus hide along.

Piaraq, their leader, had said to them, "Why do you take walrus hide along? You must not take walrus hide when you go caribou hunting. If you do, you will starve."

But they did not follow his advice. They found only a few caribou at Netchillik and had to return for want of food. After some time, some others went down Koukdjuaq to try to find the other boat's crew, who had gone along the coast of Fox Channel. When they found the crew that fall, they discovered that they too were starving. All the people, except Okowsecheak and his wife, were dead and these two only survived by eating of the bodies of those who had died.

An Unsuccessful Whale Hunt

This version is from the Kivalliq region.

Not very long ago, two boats were whaling near Niutang. One of them quickly found a whale. Suddenly the whale dove deep under the water and surfaced under one of the boats. The crew were thrown into the water and nearly drowned, but the crew of the other boat rescued them. They placed the men over the thwarts of their own boat, on their stomachs, until they had vomited all the salt water. The whale, however, was lost. That fall, the weather was very bad and the men caught no whales. They caught a caribou or two, but not enough for their needs. The whalers were starving.

As autumn wore on, ice formed in the places outside of the fiord.

They had some walrus meat on the island Lidliaajuin and made up their minds to go overland to the point nearest to it. They would cross over to the island on the ice. Etwallou was their leader. They succeeded in crossing the new ice and reached their caches.

Then Etwallou said, "Take all the meat out of the caches and divide it into equal parts."

He said so several times in order to make sure they understood. But when they reached the meat, the men could not even wait until all the stones had been removed from the cache. They were so hungry they devoured each piece of meat as soon as they saw it. When they'd had enough, they divided the remainder, slept, and, on the following day, they put the meat into a skin, put it on their backs, and carried it home.

At a place named Ichagatto, near Sikosuilaq, while the ice was forming on the ponds, a number of men were crossing a lake on their way to the caribou hunting grounds. The ice was still thin; and three of the men—Noodlooapik, Angmatcheak, and Angoomishik—broke through and were unable to get out again. Pudawallow and Mikiejew tried to throw ropes to them in order to pull them out, but the ropes were too short. The cold water soon benumbed them and they drowned.

Mikiejew ran to the shore and called his mother. She came quickly and while they hurried to the place where the men had fallen through, Mikiejew explained what had happened. Mikiejew's mother, when seeing the bodies, thought they were rocks. She tried to pull them out of the water, but she broke through herself and was only rescued with great difficulty by Pudawallow.

Keyooksaak, an old man, and his wife, Ooagejalaw, heard of what had happened. They took a pole which they knocked on the ice in front of them to test its thickness until they were near enough to the bodies to reach them with a long stick. Then they drew them back out of the ice water and took them to shore.

The old man said, "Was it not too bad for them to try to walk on the ice when it was so thin?"

Pudawallow replied, "We thought it was strong enough."
Then they all went back to their homes.

At home the old man said again, "Was it not too bad for them to try to walk on the ice when it was so thin?"

And Pudawallow and Mikiejew replied again, "Yes, but we did not know any better. We thought it was strong enough."

This version is from the Kivalliq region.

The Old Woman and her Grandchild

A long time ago the people were starving. They left their village, leaving an old woman with her granddaughter behind. As the two were very hungry, the old woman wrought a spell to induce the foxes to come to her house.

At first the caribou came. When they heard them coming, the child went out and saw a large herd of caribou. She entered the house again and told her grandmother that the caribou had come. The old woman ordered her to send them away.

Next the muskoxen came. When they heard them coming, the child went out and when she saw the muskoxen she reported to her grandmother, who told her to send them away.

Next came the wolves, but they were also sent away. They heard the tramp of more animals. The child went out and saw a large number of bears. She went in and told her grandmother, who ordered her to send them away.

The old woman said, "I want the foxes to come."

Again, they heard tramping. The child went out to see who was there and found a great number of wolverines. She told her grandmother and the old woman ordered her to send them away.

Once more they heard a noise and when the child went out, she saw a great many rabbits. She told her grandmother that the rabbits were outside. The old woman at first thought that she would like to keep them, but when she saw how lean they were she told the child to send them away.

Again they heard a noise and when the child went out, she saw a great number of foxes. She told her grandmother that the foxes were outside. The old woman asked her to invite them in, and when the whole house was full, she shut the door. The old woman took a stick and killed them all.

Then they wanted blubber for their lamp. So the grandmother took the strap from her waist and made a harpoon and a line out of it. She urinated and thus melted a hole in the ice. Soon a seal came up, which she harpooned and caught. They had plenty of blubber after that.

The old woman had all she wanted, except a man. Therefore she transformed herself into a man by making a penis out of the bone for trimming the lamp and by making her testicles out of fire stones.

Once she had become a man she wanted to go sealing. She transformed her privates into a sledge. Then she defecated and wiped herself with snow. She transformed the pieces of snow with which she had wiped herself into dogs by throwing them on the ground.

She made a kayak out of the tattooing on her forehead and a paddle out of the tattooing on her cheeks. Then she married her granddaughter, who was soon with child. One day when she was out sealing, a man came to the snow house.

When he saw the sledge, he asked, "Who made the sledge?"

"Grandmother made it."

"Who made the dogs?"

"Grandmother."

"Who made the kayak?"

"Grandmother did."

"And who is the father of your child?"

"Grandmother."

While the man was in the hut, the grandmother returned from sealing. When she looked through the entrance, she saw the man's legs. She was overcome with shame and dropped down dead.

The man wanted to take the young woman home with him and they sat down on the sledge, but when he whipped the dogs, they were transformed into snow and the sledge was changed again into what it had originally been. Then they walked on to the camp.

Soon afterwards, the young woman died.

The Woman who Could not Be Satiated

This version is from the South Baffin region.

In Akbakto lived a woman named Teneme, who had lost her husband. All the people in her village were willing to give her food, but she pretended that she wished to starve. One day, she visited Unaraw, a woman who was married to one of her relatives. Unaraw was feeding some dogs and when she happened to leave the house, Teneme took some of the food out of the kettle and ate it.

When Unaraw came in again, she asked, "Why do you eat my dogs' food, even before it is cooked?"

Teneme said, "Please give me some more, I am hungry."

But Unaraw did not give her any more.

Then Teneme went to visit other people and begged for food; but, no matter how much she was given, she always asked for more. In the evening, when the seal hunters returned, Unaraw told her husband what Teneme had been doing.

The man said, "This is dreadful, dreadful! I've never heard of any one desiring to eat dog's food all the time."

Another day, when the men were out again, Teneme visited Unaraw and stared at her intently until Unaraw became frightened, thinking that Teneme would eat her.

She moved back on the bed and Teneme asked, "Why do you move away from me? Come nearer."

But Unaraw said that she was afraid. Just at that moment a visitor came in and Teneme withdrew. In the evening, when Unaraw told her husband, the men decided to desert Teneme.

The people got ready to leave, but before they left, they barricaded the door of Teneme's house, shutting her in with her two children. After several months had passed, they thought again of Teneme and a sledge went back to look after her and her children. The man who went there saw that she had killed and eaten her children, and that she also was dead.

CHAPTER FIVE

Animals in Human Form

In this chapter, humans and animals interact in various ways, often on an equal footing. The stories clearly have a metaphoric dimension and the animals can be seen to represent human behaviour in their actions. But there is also the sense in which animals and humans are detached observers of their shared but discrete worlds.

The reader may want to be on the lookout for the following:

- ⊙ *Magic*
- ⊙ *Helping spirits*
- ⊙ *The observance of taboos*
- ⊙ *Trials*
- ⊙ *Murder*
- ⊙ *Revenge*

The Woman who Heard Bears Speak

This version is from the Netsilik region.

There was once a woman who ran away from home because she was angry with her husband. She had a baby with her in her amaut. She walked and walked and came to a house where there was no one at home. It was just like an ordinary house, so she went in. Everybody was out hunting. The woman was a shaman and she knew that the inhabitants of the house were bears in human form. They became her helping spirits from the moment she went into their home.

In the evening, when they returned from hunting, she crawled in to hide behind the sealskin hangings that lined the interior of the snow hut. The bears were great hunters and they had a well-built, big snow hut lined with beautiful sealskins. From her hiding place the woman could hear what the bears spoke about while they ate only the fat of their kill, as bears do.

The old couple and their sons ate together while the youngest of the sons, who put on airs despite his inexperience, spoke about the human practice of hunting around the breathing holes of seals, saying,

"Those shin bone figures are terribly thin on their lower halves. One almost feels inclined to knock them down."

His parents, however, remonstrated: "It's not so easy to tackle these shin bone figures. They have hunting gear and their dogs to help them."

The bears' speech sounded strange—only the woman could understand it.

The old people warned the young one to keep his head, but he did not listen. The next day he went man-hunting just the same. He was young and disobedient. Evening came and they waited in vain for his return. He had tried to attack some humans and they had killed him. Four days had passed when he finally returned with a harpoon head hanging in his fur.

He had learned that it was dangerous to attack people and he told his parents everything he had gone through. He had tried to hunt the slender shin bone figures that walked about upright on two legs, but when they set their dogs on him he had turned frightened and had run away. The dogs, however, were faster and did not become tired and out of breath. They caught up to him when he himself had to stop to get his wind and quench his thirst by eating snow. When his back was turned, they nipped his tail. As soon as they bit his tail he became strangely slack at the knees and sat down, feeling no inclination at all to run away.

In the meantime, the shin bone figures had reached him and, when they simply pointed something that looked like a rod at him, he suddenly felt a scorching heat in his body; he became so faint that he simply threw himself down on the snow. Then they all surrounded him and he got up with difficulty to run, but again the dogs nipped his tail, so he had to sit down again. Once more the men pointed at him and, inexpressibly tired, he fell over and became unconscious.

Thus the bear was killed by the humans and they gave him a death taboo that was as it should be; for four days his soul rested among many splendid presents in the house of the humans. Then he was free again and could go back home, rich in experience and with great respect for the shin bone figures whom he had previously despised.

The woman ran away from the house of the bears and told the people of her village what she had gone through. This story illustrates how important it is for a dead bear's soul to receive the proper taboo. For the strongest thing of all life here on Earth is the soul.

The Man who Took a Wife from Among the Wild Geese

This version is from Northern Greenland (Polar Inuit).

A man once saw a huge flock of wild geese in the middle of a large lake. The geese had thrown off their feather coats and turned into men and women, and they were bathing and playing about in the water.

He was seized with a desire to take two of them for wives, so he hid their coats; but as he sprang forward and caught them, one of them wept so bitterly that he gave her coat back. The other he brought home with him to his grandmother and made his wife.

She soon gave him twins, both boys.

But the wild goose grew homesick for her own kind and began to collect bird's feathers and wings. She soon had enough feathers to make a feather suit for herself.

One day, when her husband was out seal catching, she made herself a coat of feathers and flew away with her children.

When her husband came home, he set off running at once to seek them. Because he did not have a coat of feathers he could not fly as his wife and children had.

On the way, he met with two earth spirits, who were tearing each other's hair out. They placed themselves in his way, but he flew over them by magic, for he was a great magician. Next he met with two hillock spirits that were trampling upon one another. They too blocked his way, but he flew over them by magic.

Then he came to a pot that had seal's flesh boiling in it and the pot was talking to itself, saying, "A man po-po-po."

The pot wanted to entice him to eat, but he flew over it by magic again. Then came to a litter of hairless puppy dogs that also wished to prevent him passing. They were the earth's dogs, hairless, like worms. He passed them by and went on to Kajungajorssuaq, a man whose buttocks were horribly deformed.

The magician, who knew his thoughts and knew that he was ashamed of his appearance, approached him from the front.

"How did you come?" asked Kajungajorssuaq.

"I came this way," replied the man.

"Good, if you had come up from behind me, I would have killed you. You shall go on to the people that you are seeking; I can hear them from here." He showed him the way.

The magician shut his eyes and leaped down onto an ice floe. In this way he floated across the water to his wife and children.

As he approached them, his children saw him. "Father has come," they called out.

"I will see him, bring him in," said the wife. And he went in.

She, in the meantime, had taken another husband, an old fellow, who at once took flight.

"Let me get out: I am felling unwell, qoa-r-r-rit!" he cried and rushed out through the passage. He was an old long-tailed duck.

The man and wife then lived together again, but the wife did not care for her old husband. So one day she pretended to die.

The husband buried her, but as soon as he left the burial site she broke out of the cairn.

"I saw Mother over there," the children began to cry out.

"Oh! Then let us look at her," replied the man, and he looked out of the window.

"Who are you?" he asked.

"I am Qitdluk," she lied.

So then he harpooned his wife in his anger.

When the murder became known, his wife's friends, the wild geese, flew away.

But the man, who thought that they would come back again to take their revenge, went again to Kajungajorssuaq and he gave him a long, heavy whip.

Then one day, the geese came into sight and he knew they were there to avenge his murdered wife. They drew near like a great cloud; but he lashed at their plumage and killed them.

Only a few escaped. But they came again—a larger flock of them—and he thrashed them all to death.

After that, the man lived for a long time on all the fat wild geese.

This version is from Northern Greenland (Polar Inuit).

The Man who Took a Fox for a Wife

There was, once upon a time, a man who thought he would like to take a wife who was not like everybody else's wife. So he caught a little fox and took her with him to his tent.

One day, when he had been out seal catching, he came home and surprised his little wife, who had changed into a woman. Her tail had become a lovely big knot of hair on her head. She had also taken off her shaggy skin. And when he saw her like that he thought her very beautiful. After that, she began to wish to see other people, so they went away and settled down elsewhere.

One of the other men in their new camp had taken a little hare as his wife. The two men thought they would like to exchange wives and they did so.

But the man who had borrowed the little fox wife despised her when he had lain down beside her. She smelt so strongly of fox that it was unpleasant.

The fox became angry because she was so anxious to please

men; she put out the lamp with her tail, sprang out of the house, and fled far away into the hills.

Up in the hills she found a worm and stayed with him.

But her husband, who was fond of her, went after her and found her at last with the worm, who had clothed himself in human shape.

The man could see that the worm's face was all burnt and he knew instantly that the worm was his mortal enemy. Long ago, the man had burnt a worm and that worm's soul had become the man who was standing before him.

The worm then challenged the man, and suggested that they arm wrestle. They wrestled, and the man found the worm very easy to vanquish. Once he had defeated the worm, he went out and would not have anything more to do with his wife.

He started off on his travels and came to the sand dwellers. They had houses on the beach by the seashore, just at the turning of the tide.

Their houses were quite small and they themselves were dwarfs. They were so small they called eider ducks walruses, as small things appeared very large to them. Other than their size they looked just like men. They were quite harmless.

When the man saw their houses, which had roofs of stone, he

went into them, but he had to make himself quite small; he was a very great magician, so this was easily done.

And as soon as he entered, they brought out meat: a whole shoulder of a large walrus. In reality, it was only the wing of an eider duck. And they began to eat greedily of it, but they did not eat it all.

After he had stayed for a time with these people, he went back to his own house. People never see beings like these small men anymore, but our forefathers told us of them; they knew them.

Ititaujang

This version is from the South Baffin region.

One day a man, while out caribou hunting in the interior of the country, heard the cries of women. Although he searched everywhere, he could not see anyone. Finally he came in sight of a small lake, in which he saw four women bathing. They had taken off their boots and their jackets. The man hid behind some high ground for a time and then crept up to the lake cautiously. On the shore he found the women's clothes, which he took.

The women observed him. They cried and asked him for their clothes. He returned clothes to three of the women, but those of the last one he kept. The other women put on their boots and jackets, and at once they were transformed into geese and flew away.

The remaining woman asked again and again for her jacket. Instead of giving it to her, he merely asked, "Will you be my wife?"

She did not reply, but only asked for her jacket.

He said again, "Will you be my wife?"

She retorted, "They have all left me. Give me my jacket."

Again he asked her, "Will you be my wife?" And finally she consented, but still continued to ask for her jacket.

He said, "Do you really want to be my wife?"

"Indeed, I will," she answered. Then he asked her to go home with him and they lived together as husband and wife.

After some time she gave birth to a boy. When the boy was large enough to walk about, the people of the village caught a whale. They were all carrying the meat ashore, the goose-woman among them, when suddenly she noticed some of the blood of the whale on her dress. Then she began to cry. She left the people, took her child, and went along the beach. Soon she found some feathers, which she placed between her fingers and between those of the boy. At once, both were transformed into geese and flew away.

The people who had seen the transformation called to the man, whose name was Ititaujang, and told him that his wife and child were flying away. He immediately left the whale and followed them to the land of the birds, away beyond the horizon.

After he had travelled for some time, he saw two large rocks which shut and opened. He tried to go around them, for fear of being caught in between, but he was unable to do so and had to pass between them. After he had succeeded in passing the rocks, he went on and came to two wolves, one on each side of his path. The wolves were eating something. He tried to go around them, but was unable to do so. He had to rush through between them. He went on and came to a large pot full of boiling meat. He could not go around it, but had to pass over it and was nearly scalded. He continued on and came to a large lamp. He could not go around it and had to step across it.

After walking for a long time, he saw a man's pelvis lying on the ground. He tried to go around it, but he had to have intercourse with it and only then could he step right over it.

After he had passed this last obstacle, he travelled on for a long time.

Finally, he saw a man. When he looked at the man, he noticed that he could look through his body. He had no insides. Ititaujang became frightened, and went around, approaching the man from behind. The man's name was Ixalu'qdjung. He was standing at the bank of a brook, chopping chips from a piece of red wood with his hatchet. There was also a piece of white wood lying by his side.

When Ititaujang approached him, Ixalu'qdjung asked, "Where do you come from?"

The traveller replied, "I come from that direction," pointing towards Ixalu'qdjung's back.

The latter rejoined, "If you had come the other way, I should have killed you with my hatchet."

He did not want anyone to see that he had no insides.

Then Ititaujang asked, "Do you know where my wife is?"

Ixalu'qdjung replied, "Listen!"

They heard distant voices with that of Ititaujang's lost wife among them. The people were on the other side of the river. Ititaujang asked Ixalu'qdjung to help him cross the river, which was very deep. Then Ixalu'qdjuag cut off a piece of wood and gave it to him.

He said, "This is your kayak; shut your eyes and do not open them until you reach the other shore."

Ititaujang closed his eyes and the piece of wood turned into a kayak around him. But when he was some distance from shore, he opened his eyes a little. At once the kayak disappeared under him; but when he shut his eyes again, he found himself again in his kayak.

Finally, he reached the other shore and travelled until he saw some huts. Then he saw a boy coming towards him, and recognized his son.

The boy ran back to the hut and said to his mother, "Father is coming!"

But his mother merely said, "He will never find us here."

The boy ran back to his father, who said to him, "Tell my wife to come here."

The boy ran back again and said to his mother, "Father has arrived. He wants you to come and see him."

The mother said to the boy, "Go and tell him not to come here. The ground here is boiling."

By that time, the man had arrived at the door of the hut and entered. Inside he saw his wife and an old man.

The old man said, "Bring me the chest with the feathers."

The woman gave him the chest; and as soon as he took it, the woman, the child, and the old man were transformed into birds. Ititaujang became very angry. He took his knife and cut open his wife's belly while she was flying away, and many eggs fell from her stomach.

This version is from the South Baffin region.

Dialogue between Two Ravens

Father: My son, my son, always be on the lookout for men.
Son: There is a person away there.

Father: Where is he?

Son: By the side of a great iceberg.

Father: My son, my son, always be on the lookout for men.

Son: There is a person away there.

Father: Where is he?

Son: There in front of us.

Father: My son, my son, always be on the lookout for men.

Son: There is a person away there.

Father: Where is he?

Son: Just beyond the point of land.

Father: My son, my son, always be on the lookout for men.

Son: There is a person away there.

Father: Where is he?

Son: This side of the point.

Father: My son, my son, always be on the lookout for men.

Son: There is a person coming.

Father: Where is he?

Son: Just beyond the beach.

Father: My son, my son, always be on the lookout for men.

Son: There is a person away there.

Father: Where is he?

Son: He is in the entrance of our dwelling.

So the raven told his son to go and look for men and he discovered a man at the door of their house.

The man entered and saw the father who said, "Haak! Surely you are hungry. We are generally hungry when we wander away from home."

He asked his son to bring in some human flesh. The boy brought it in. The old man cut off a piece and gave it to the hunter.

The hunter said, "I do not like that kind of flesh."

The old man retorted, "Give it to me, I can eat it."

After he had finished eating, he said to the boy, "Bring in some whale skin." But what he brought was really fowl's dung.

He again gave it to the hunter, who said he could not eat it.

"Give it to me," said the old man, "I can eat it."

Then he told the boy to bring in scrapings of whale bone. He offered this to the hunter, who said he could not eat it.

The old man said again, "I can eat it. Give it to me." But after he had finished eating he said, "My stomach aches," and he vomited everything he had eaten.

The hunter left the house of the raven and, a short distance away, there was the house of the Gull. The hunter was invited to enter. He went in and the Gull gave him dried salmon, which he was glad to eat. Then he left, went home, and told how the birds had fed him.

The Man who Married the Fox

This version is from the South Baffin region.

Once upon a time, there was a man who went out sealing, while his wife went to gather heather. But when he came home in the evening, he found that she had gathered very little. After some time the man became suspicious that there might be some reason why she did not gather more heather than she did; but he dismissed the matter from his mind. When she continued to bring only small quantities of heather home, his suspicions grew.

One day, when he had plenty of seal meat and blubber, so that he did not need to go hunting, he made up his mind to follow the woman. He saw her going to a small pond.

When she reached the pond, she threw small stones into it, shouting, "Come and show your penis!"

After she had continued to call to the pond and throw stones into it for some time, a man's penis appeared above the water. She took off her boots and trousers, placed it between her legs and pleasured herself with it. When she was finished, the penis disappeared again into the pond.

This is the penis of the lake's inua (indweller). An inua is an anthropomorphic representation of something's essence. This is a very common concept in Inuit myths and legends.

The woman put on her clothes and went back home. When she was gone, her husband did as he had seen his wife doing. He took off his clothes, threw stones into the water, and called upon the penis to show itself. After some time, it appeared. Then he cut it off with his knife and the whole pond became red with blood.

He put on his clothes, went home, and found his wife outside the hut. She had lit a fire and was cooking seal meat. The man did not speak to her about what he had seen and done; but when she went into the hut to fetch something, he threw the man's penis into the boiling kettle among the seal meat. After a while, when the meat was done, the man took the penis out of the pot, and handed it to his wife.

She did not recognize it but, since it did not taste like seal meat, she asked her husband, "What is this that I am eating here? It is not seal meat."

"Why," he replied, "it is your lover's penis."

She simply shouted, "Oof! It is much better than young seal."

The man made up his mind to take revenge upon his faithless wife. One day he pretended to go out hunting but, instead of searching for seals, he collected in his mitten all kinds of spiders, beetles, and other bugs. When he came home, he secretly placed the mitten filled with insects under the blanket on the bed. In the evening, when they went to bed, the insects came out of the mitten and crawled into all the openings of the woman. They made holes through the thinner parts of her skin and crawled into her body. They ate her up entirely and crawled out of her ears, nose, and mouth. Thus she died.

Her husband buried her, covering her body with whale ribs and stones. He lived all alone for a long time.

One day, when he arrived home in the evening from sealing, he found that someone had cooked seal meat for him, which was still warm. He was much surprised, not knowing who had done it.

Another day, returning from the hunt, he again found cooked seal meat. It was quite hot, but he did not see anybody.

The third day, when he returned, the seal meat was still boiling, but there was no sign of a woman. Another day, upon his return from hunting, he saw a pretty young woman coming from his wife's grave. She did not see him. She went to his hut and began to stretch a fox skin outside of the hut. Then she went back to the grave.

As soon as she was out of sight, the man took the fox skin from the drying frame. The woman felt at once when he touched it, for it was her own skin that she was drying.

She came forth and asked for the skin; but he simply replied, "You are my wife now."

The raven couple is in human form.

But she remained silent and asked again for her fox skin, saying, "Give me my fox skin; it has a bad smell."

The man kept the skin and said, "You shall be my wife."

She did not give any answer, but merely asked again for her fox skin, saying that it had a bad smell.

The man replied, "You shall be my wife and if I should notice a strong smell, I will not mention it."

The woman persisted in asking for her fox skin. The man asked her again, "Will you be my wife?"

This time she consented, speaking in a low voice, but again asked him for her fox skin. Then the man repeated his request for her to become his wife. This time she freely consented. Then he invited her to go into the hut and when she again asked for her fox skin, he gave it to her. They lived for some time in the hut and they loved each other.

After some time, a Raven and his wife came and erected their hut nearby. In time the two families became very friendly.

One day, the Raven said to the man, "Let us exchange wives."

The man objected for a long time, but finally yielded to the Raven's persistent requests. He asked the Raven to promise not to mention anything about a smell, if he noticed that his wife smelled strongly. Then they exchanged their wives for the night. They went to bed, but the fox-woman did not allow the Raven to touch her.

Finally, he grew angry, turned his back on her and said, "What a bad smell there is!"

Then the woman began to cry. She arose and took a small fox skin from a small bag she had with her. She began to rub and to chew it in order to soften it, intending to put on the skin; but, since she was in a hurry to put it on, she did not stop to finish the legs of the skin. Then she put it on and the Raven saw only a fox running out of the house. The Raven regretted that he had broken his promise and was afraid that he might lose his own wife in exchange for one he had just lost.

Meanwhile, the Raven's wife had been with the fox's husband. He found that her body was covered with dirt and that she smelled very bad.

Finally, he shouted, "Oh, how bad you smell!"

Then he went out of his hut and he saw the footprints of his wife in the snow. She had not had time to put her hands and her feet into the fox's skin and had, for this reason, retained her hands, her human feet, and her boots. He followed her tracks and found that they ended at a small hole in the stones of an old hut. He stamped his foot over the hole and called her. Although she knew it was her husband calling, she spoke as though addressing her children.

"Go out and see who is there."

Then an insect came out of the hole.

When the insect appeared, the man said to it, "Smoke is coming out of your head."

In this way quite a number of insects and worms were sent out of the hole and to each of them he said the same. Finally, his wife asked him to come in. She told him to shut his eyes, to turn both sides of his jacket inward, and to come in backward. He complied with her instructions and backed into the fox's hole. When he got inside, he saw a large dog in one corner of the fox's den. It was his son in the form of a dog. His wife appeared to him again in human shape, as he had known her. The fox's hole seemed to him like a hut.

The Boy who Lived on Ravens

This version is from the South Baffin region.

Many people lived at Niutang. One time, when they were quarrelling, they murdered a man who had not intended to kill anyone.

After he was buried, his widow lived all by herself and subsisted upon the little that people gave her. After some time, they moved to Katsag, leaving the woman behind. The night before they left, one of the men went into her hut and slept with her and she thanked him for having visited.

The widow was with child, and soon the child was born. They had very little food. One day, while she was walking close to the house which she had built for herself, she saw a great many ravens go into it. She took up a stick, went in to the house, and killed them all except for one, which tried to escape from her by jumping to and fro. She tried to catch it, but the raven became smaller and smaller, until she could hardly see it; after many attempts, however, she succeeded in killing it. Then she put the ravens outside to freeze. With all those ravens to eat, she and her son had enough to live on for some time.

When the supply was nearly exhausted, she went out again and soon saw a great many ravens going into her hut. She did as before— fastened the door and killed the birds.

The woman and her son lived entirely on raven meat.

The boy grew up very quickly and soon was able to go sealing. One day, when he returned from a sealing trip, his mother discovered that his face looked quite black. He had been living on raven meat and had become himself like a raven. After seeing that, his mother thought of avenging the death of her husband.

She said to her boy, "I think you are now able to look out for yourself. You must avenge the death of your father."

Then the boy replied, "I want to go and see those people who killed him."

Before he set out, his mother took the body of a dog and positioned it as though it were alive. She opened its mouth, so that the animal looked like a very fierce dog that wanted to bite people. The mother used the dog to foresee whether they would be successful against their enemies. She said, "I will set up the body of the dog. If it stands up, we will go, if it falls down, we will stay here."

They put the dog down and it stood as though it were alive. Then they left and built a house not far from the shore, close to the men who had killed the boy's father.

The boy had made a great many arrows, and early in the morning he said to his mother, "Go on shore and tell those men to come here. Tell them that I am ready to be awakened. But do not go into the houses, only call them through the windows."

The woman went and stepped up to the windows while the people were still in bed and said, "My son sends me to tell you to come down to him. He is ready to be awakened."

Then she went back. The men jumped up and went down to the ice. They were intending to kill the boy who had set up the dog near his hut. The men began to shoot their arrows at him, but he dodged them, jumping about like a raven. When they had spent all their arrows, the boy ran between the men and the village and began to kill them with his arrows. On the following day, when the bodies of his enemies were all frozen, he arranged them as if they were alive and then went to his mother and told her to look at them. They looked just like people sealing on the ice. He then took one of the women as his wife and went to live in Niutang.

The Visitor

This version is from the South Baffin region.

In Kingnait lived a man by the name of Attongey, who wanted to travel through the country with a large team of dogs. He made some harnesses and went to a place where there were a number of good-sized stones, some red, some white, some brown, and some speckled. He decided to harness the stones and transform them into dogs to be used on his journey.

When he was ready to start, he cried out, "Haa, haa, haa, Attongey! Haa, haa, haa, Attongey, Attongey!"

At once the stones were transformed into dogs, which came at his call. He fastened them to his sledge and started off. After he had gone a long distance from home, he arrived at a village. There he stopped and fed his dogs. Two old women came down from the houses to see him. They wanted a little of the meat that the dogs were being fed and picked up some meat from the ground.

Then Attongey spoke to them and said, "You are like ravens."

At once the women jumped like ravens and cried "Qaq!" Again they picked at the meat.

Attongey hit them with a stick, saying, "Go away from here if you are ravens."

They went home at once. One of the old women was quite angry at the treatment she had received, but she did not say so to Attongey.

After Attongey had fed his dogs and put his harnesses in order, he went up to the huts and entered one of them. Meanwhile, the old woman whom he had whipped took the brains of a man and of a wolf and mixed them together. Then she sent her granddaughter to the hut where Attongey was staying to ask for some blood to mix with the brains.

She told the girl not to say what she wanted it for, but the girl, who was very young, said, "Please give me some blood. Grandmother told me not to tell you that she is going to mix it with the brains of a man and of a wolf."

She obtained the blood and carried it to her grandmother. When the old woman had mixed the blood and the brains together, she told the girl to invite the stranger to the house. Attongey accepted the invitation.

When he arrived, the old woman handed him the mixture she had prepared, telling him to eat it all. He sat down and ate it all. Then he put the dish in which the food had been given to him between his legs

When he took it away it was full. He passed it to the old woman and ordered her to eat it. She was sure that she saw him eat all the brains and so she thought that he had vomited onto the plate and offered it to her. She ate it and then put the plate between her legs. When she took it away it was still empty. When she saw that it was empty, she put it back between her legs; and when she took it away again, it was still empty. The old woman tried again and again to make food appear on the plate as the man had done, but always found the plate empty. She died soon after.

The people of the village had plenty of sledges, but no dogs. Attongey resolved to escape from them. Therefore, one night he cut the lashings with which the bars of the sledges were tied to the runners. He cut them on the lower side of the bars on the inside of the runners, so that the people would not notice what he had done. Then he got his dog sledge ready and, when all was done, he re-entered the snow house and played cup-and-ball with the people. The carving that they were using was very pretty. First he sat down while playing with it, but after a while he arose, went out with it, and started off. Soon he was quite a distance away from the place. The people jumped on their sledges and followed after him.

They drove their sledges along with sticks. They very nearly caught up with Attongey and they cried out, "Give us our cup-and-ball!"

When they came quite close to Attongey, their sledges broke down, because of the broken lashings. Attongey made considerable headway before his pursuers had repaired their runners. Once more they nearly caught up with Attongey, when their sledges broke down again. In their eagerness of pursuit, they had only placed the crossbars on the runners, without properly lashing them. Again they repaired the sledges and followed. By this time Attongey was far ahead. Eventually they gained ground and were close beside him, but the sledges broke down again. At last they gave up the pursuit and returned home.

Attongey finally reached his own village.

The Woman who Transformed herself into a Bear

This version is from the South Baffin region.

Quite a number of Inuit lived at Nugumiut during the winter, but during other seasons they moved camp to a place more suitable for hunting, or where they could be nearer their game.

There is a tradition concerning an old woman who had been left alone at this place with her granddaughter, a young girl about six years old. The old woman's son and his wife had moved to another place, where they lived all by themselves. Left all alone, the old woman and her granddaughter searched the huts for something to eat. At last they found a piece of bearskin from the face of a bear. There was no flesh on it.

One day, the grandmother said to the girl, "We will go away and try to find your parents."

They started out, but the girl soon grew tired. They rested awhile.

Then the old woman said to the girl, "Go on ahead. Do not be afraid. If you should meet a bear, walk up to it and sit on its back."

The girl went on. When she was out of sight, her grandmother transformed herself into a bear, which followed the girl. When the girl saw it, she stopped and the bear walked up to her. She sat down on its back and they travelled on in the direction of the place where the girl's father and mother lived. At dark, the bear reached the ground ice. The girl slipped off the bear's back.

Then the bear spoke. "When you are with your father and mother in their house, tell them that I should like to come inside during the night, as it is cold on the ice at night."

When the girl had gone, the bear resumed the form of the old woman.

The child went to her mother's porch and said, "Grandmother has come. May she come in during the night, for it is very cold outside?"

The girl's father refused admittance to his mother.

Then the child went back to the old woman, who asked her, "What did your father say?"

"He said 'don't come here,'" replied the child.

The grandmother told the girl to tell him that her grandmother wanted to come in for a drink.

The father said, "No. She shall not come in here."

The girl went back to her grandmother and told her what her father said.

The old woman replied, "Tell him that grandmother is hungry and wants to come in."

The girl obeyed; but her father replied, "She shall not come in here."

The girl went and told her grandmother. Then the grandmother whipped her with a small piece of rope and thus transformed her granddaughter into a bear. She also transformed herself into a bear. They both went up to the hut and broke into it. The man tried to kill the bears, first with his harpoon, then with his spear, and finally with his knife; but all his weapons broke and the bears killed both him and his wife.

The Woman who Became a Bear and Killed her Enemy

This version is from the South Baffin region.

In Saumia lived an old woman named Analookashaw, who had a foster son who was her only support. One day, the young man went off sealing with a man named Pupewalow. While the two men were out together, Pupewalow suggested that they should try their strength in a wrestling match. While they were wrestling, Pupewalow stabbed and killed the young man. It was known that Pupewalow had a grudge against the young man whom he had killed. Pupewalow did not mention to anyone that he had seen or killed the youth.

The old woman was waiting for her foster son, and when he did not come, she went to Pupewalow's hut and asked him where he had left her boy. Pupewalow said he had not seen him.

On the following day, the other men said to Pupewalow, "What did you do with Analookashaw's son? Where did you leave him?"

But Pupewalow only said he had not seen him.

When the young man did not return, the people thought that he had died. Analookashaw believed that Pupewalow had killed her son, although no one had told her this.

She went to his house and said, "Is my son dead? Did you stab him or kill him?"

He denied his guilt, but she knew that he had killed him because she was an angakkuq.

She continued, "Tell me if you stabbed him with your knife."

But he replied, "I did not stab him, nor did I wish to do any such thing."

Analookashaw went home.

Some time later, Pupewalow caught a bear, the meat of which was consumed, except a small part which was left on the skull. Analookashaw quietly approached the bear carcass and stole the skull without being noticed by the hunter. She removed all the flesh from the head of the bear, put the skull into her hood, walked around all the huts, and finally entered Pupewalow's hut.

Then she addressed him, saying, "Tell me, now. You did kill my son."

She was close to his legs and rested her arms on his knees. Then she opened her mouth with her hands and asked Pupewalow to look and see that her teeth had been almost worn down and that many were missing.

She said, "I shall die soon and my soul will enter a bear. It will come and devour you if you do not confess that you killed my son. If you confess, I will not wish to die and you will be saved the wrath of my avenging spirit."

She moved about the hut as she spoke and Pupewalow saw the bear skull in her hood. He realized that Analookashaw intended to bring it to life and have it devour him for killing her son. All the people of the camp could hear the old woman in Pupewalow's hut, and they gathered round to see what was happening.

The other people became suspicious and said, "Certainly he did kill Analookashaw's son." But Pupewalow would not confess.

During the same winter, the old woman died and was buried. One day in spring, Pupewalow and another man were sealing, sitting at the breathing holes of seals not far away from the winter village. Analookashaw's soul had gone into a bear, which was sitting near the ground ice. The bear was trying to find Pupewalow, but since it couldn't see him from the ground ice, it went up the hill. There, the bear discovered him sitting at the seal hole and it moved down the hill slowly until it came to Pupewalow. Suddenly Pupewalow's friend saw the bear and shouted to Pupewalow to look out, but Pupewalow did not understand him.

The man shouted a second time, "The bear is close to you. Look out!"

This time Pupewalow understood and looked up; but at the same moment the bear jumped at him and knocked him down. As soon as he arose, it knocked him down again. His friend ran to assist him, but the bear had already killed him and torn him up. His friend did not venture near, but turned and ran home as fast as he could. He told the people of the camp what he had seen.

Those on shore had seen the bear killing Pupewalow and all ran away except Pupewalow's son and his adopted son. They took up their bows and arrows, intending to kill the bear. Pupewalow's son shot at the bear several times with his arrows, but missed. Then he asked his foster brother to shoot at the bear. The boy hit it in the right leg and then shot it in the heart. When the bear was dead the people returned.

They saw that the bear's skin was worn and old.

Someone said, "Do not skin it. It is not good because it has killed a man."

Then they went to the place where Pupewalow had been killed. They found his body all torn to pieces. They tried to track the bear, to discover where it had come from. They traced it first to the hilltop and from there to the ground ice. The first tracks were human, but gradually they changed into bear's tracks. After three nights the body of the bear began to move and the people were afraid that it might arise again. Pupewalow's son cut off its legs with a knife and threw the legs in different directions. Then the bear did not move again.

The Fox

This version is from the South Baffin region.

A man named Neqingoaq went out to tend to a fox trap.

As he walked, he heard a fox that was caught in the trap sing, "Oh, why did you put the bait in the trap, my son Neqingoaq? This flat stone is in my way. Pray, come and take it away."

Neqingoaq's mother had died, and when the fox sang to him and called him son he was very much surprised.

He let the animal go at once.

This version is from the South Baffin region.

The Woman who Became a Raven

The husband of a woman named Peqaq was angry with her. After they had argued for some time, she left her home, walking on the ice and weeping bitterly.

Her husband followed her on his sledge and when she saw him, she said, "Oh, that I might become a raven!"

She was turned into a raven and flew to the top of an iceberg. Her husband drove along the side of the iceberg, but since he did not see his wife, he returned home.

As soon as the man had returned home, the raven flew away and in the evening alighted on a rock near Niutang.

The people were surprised and said to each other, "What is that on top of the rock? Is it the moon?"

"Oh," said some, "it is a person."

When these people went to sleep, the raven flew down from the rock. She peeped through a hole in a tent and saw a man in the rear.

She thought, "Oh, that he might come out and relieve himself!"

She had hardly thought so, when the man put on his garments and went out to relieve himself. The raven had resumed the shape of a woman and when he saw her, he was very pleased with her and took her as his wife.

Story of Three Girls

This version is from the Kivalliq region.

Three girls were at play near the beach. When they saw a whale blowing, one of them said jokingly, "I will take the whale for my husband."

The second one looked up and saw a large eagle.

She said, "I will take the eagle for my husband."

The third one, pointing to a large boulder, said, "I will take the boulder for my husband."

While saying so, she went up to the boulder and put her hands on top of it. When she moved to walk away she was not able to take her hands off the boulder.

The eagle came down and carried one of the girls to its nest on a high cliff and the whale carried off the third one to an island. The whale gave the bones of his body to the girl to build a house and thus she was able to live in the water with her husband or on the land in her house, wherever she pleased.

One day the father and the brothers of this girl came in their boat to an island. When she saw them coming, she told her husband that she wished to go to the island. The whale, who was afraid that he might lose her, fastened a line around her and then let her swim back to the island. When she reached the island, she took the line off and tied it to one of her buckles. The girl's father used his magic to give the buckle the power to speak.

Soon the whale shouted and asked her, "Are you ready to come back?"

The buckle replied, "After a little while."

The whale called again.

Again the buckle replied, "I cannot come yet."

Then the whale became angry and hauled in the line; and when he saw there was only a buckle attached to it, he flew into a rage, swam ashore, tore the house down, and put the bones back into his body. But in his fury he forgot to take his breast bone and hip bone. Meanwhile, the father and the brother, who had taken away the young woman, had a long head start. But the whale set out in pursuit. After a while he was drawing near. Then the father of the young woman told her to throw her boots into the sea.

When the whale came near, he stopped and struck the boots with his tail until they fell to pieces. Then he continued his pursuit. When he came near, she threw her jacket into the sea. Again the whale stopped and struck the jacket until it was torn.

The girl continued throwing articles of clothing into the sea, and as the whale stopped to destroy each of them the family continued paddling away. When all her clothes were thrown away, they found themselves close to the shore. They pulled the boat over a reef and soon landed. The whale, intent on pursuit, did not notice the reef and became stranded. When the tide went out, the people killed the whale without difficulty.

The father and the brothers of the second girl, who had been carried away by the eagle, also set out to rescue her. Whenever the eagle was away caribou hunting, she worked on a rope made of caribou leg sinews. When she saw her father and her brothers coming, she told the eagle that there were a great many caribou in a certain place far away. The eagle believed her and flew away to hunt the caribou. Then she finished the rope, which was now long enough to reach down to the water. She let the rope down and her father and her brothers took hold of the end. She climbed down, was taken into the boat, and they returned home.

When the eagle came home and found that she was gone, he flew to the village and tried to recover her. He broke the window of her father's house with his wings, but her father shot him with an arrow and killed him.

Even up to present day, people point out the eagle's cliff. They say that the people used to cut off pieces from the rope until it was out of reach.

The third girl, who had married the boulder, was unable to let go, and so she gradually turned into stone. But, as long as she was alive, people brought her food.

This version is from the South Baffin region.

The Fox and the Wolf

A fox and a wolf were living at Sikosuilaq. The wolf's children used to visit the fox's children, and whenever they did so, they were given caribou fat to eat.

At one time, the fox had nothing to eat for herself and her children. When the young wolves called, the old fox said to them, "Come in and look at the fat that I am chewing!"

The young wolf said, "Let it fall down."

The fox let it fall and said, "It is just like a hammer."

Then she said, "It is like a white stone."

She asked the young wolf to eat it. After a while the young wolf went home and told his mother what had happened.

When the father wolf heard what had happened he shouted so that the fox would hear it, "Your meat is all stone. Why did you fool my child?"

The old fox-woman replied, "I did not fool your child."

Then the wolves began to cry, for they found out that all their own caribou meat had become stone. They were forced to leave their home because they had nothing to eat. Thus the fox got all the caribou meat of the wolves.

The Bear Country

This version is from the South Baffin region.

One evening, in Cumberland Sound, the children heard sealers coming home. An orphan was among the children.

They said, "Your father is not among these sealers. He is still away off."

The children went to meet the sledges of the sealers. They said again to the orphan, "Your father is left behind."

Then the orphan boy went out looking for his father. He finally came to a place where a bear had been carved up. The boy was crying because he could not find his father. It was dark by this time. He continued travelling until finally he reached the end of the land floe. At the edge of the land floe, he noticed bear tracks. He also saw a kayak coming, although it was midwinter. He waited until it reached the floe edge. The hunter asked the boy to accompany him to his village. The boy agreed, sat down on the top of the kayak, and they went away.

After a while they reached the village and the boy stayed there for three years. He grew to be quite large and learned to hunt seals.

One day, one of the men said to the boy, "You have a mother and she needs you. You had better return home. Let her know that you are still alive. When you reach home, take off your jacket because they may think you are a bear. You have been in the bear country these three years."

Then the boy started homeward and met the sealers. When they saw him, they thought he was a bear and went to attack him; but the boy took off his bearskin jacket behind a hummock and showed himself. Then they recognized him. They went home and he went right to his mother's hut.

She asked, "Who are you? It is terrible that a stranger should have arrived at my hut."

Then he answered that he was her son.

The Country of the Bears and Wolves

This version is from the South Baffin region.

A boat's crew went travelling along the north shore of Hudson Strait and reached a village.

Two children were on the beach. Suddenly they noticed the boat. Then they ran back to the huts and told their parents that strangers were coming. The people went to meet them and sang some songs. While they were singing, an old man noticed a young girl in the boat who had been looking at him the whole time. He asked her parents to give her to him as his wife.

The boat's crew travelled on, leaving the girl behind. After the boat had left, the old man fastened a thong around the girl's waist, so that, when she was out of his sight, he could still pull her and prevent her escape. They lived there in the camp for some time, and the couple had a child; but the old man always kept the young woman tied to the thong. Since he was the head man among his people, they did not dare to interfere, although they had much sympathy for the young woman.

One day the people invited him to partake of a seal that had just been caught. While he was away, the young woman escaped and followed the route that her friends from the boat had travelled. When the man discovered that his wife was not there, he destroyed his whole house looking for her.

It was winter and the woman walked along on the ice. She travelled for days, carrying her child on her back. Finally she saw a house and she was asked to enter. There were only women inside. The women said that their husbands were out hunting and they would not be home until evening. She was given something to eat and invited to lie down and sleep. She pretended to be asleep and overheard the women talking among themselves.

The one to whom the house belonged said to another one, "She is asleep now. Stab her."

As soon as she heard this, she pinched her child and pretended to be awakened by its cries. She continued to pinch the child, making it cry continually. Then she said to the women that the child would not stop crying unless she left the house and walked back and forth with it outside. She went out and as soon as she was outside, she made her escape. The women, she realized, were actually wolves.

She went on along the shore and finally came to another house. She entered and, although there were provisions and furnishings in the house, there was no one to be seen. After a while she heard someone coming. She was afraid and hid under the lining of the snow house. For fear that her child would make a noise, she smothered it with her hand.

When the people came in, she heard them say, "I smell something. A person must be here."

These people were bears. Early the next morning they took their breakfast and went off sealing; soon after they had gone, the woman escaped, leaving the body of her child behind. She walked on for many days and finally came to a place where people had camped the day before. The only thing that was left in the former camp was the receptacle for the sealing line on the kayak.

After some time she saw two kayaks coming. The men had come back to get a line holder that they had forgotten in the camp. When they discovered the woman, they asked her where she had come from. When she told them who she was, she learned that her father and mother had just moved the day before to Resolution Island. She lay down on top of one of the kayaks and was taken over to the island.

The Muskox

This version is from the Kivalliq region.

In olden times, there were two musk oxen who had taken off their skins. They sat and rubbed their skins to soften them while singing the praises of their country—how beautiful the land was, that they could always see the sun, and that the sea was a long ways off.

While they were singing, they heard a pack of dogs. At once they put on their skins and went up a hill where they thought they could defend themselves from the dogs. But soon after they reached the top of the hill, the hunters came and killed them. The men had heard their song, which is still sung today.

The Country of the Wolves

This version is from the Kivalliq region.

While two men were out sealing, the ice broke up and they drifted about for a number of days. Finally the men reached the shore. They saw two snow houses; one man went into each of the houses. One of these houses was large and the man who entered there was at once attacked by the inhabitants and devoured. Although they looked like people, the inhabitants were wolves. The other man found only a woman, whose name was Ouearnacsuneark.

As he entered, she said, "I smell a man."

When she looked up and discovered her visitor, she became very angry; but he gave her a knife as a present, and asked her to befriend him and give the knife as a present to her husband when he came home. Then she hid the man under the bedding and put his boots over the lamp to dry.

Soon one of the young people from the other large house came in.

When he entered, he said, "I smell a man!"

But the woman replied, "You smell only some old meat."

After a little while, the young man went out again and told the people in his house that he thought another person must have arrived and must have entered the second house.

His mother went over to the house of their neighbours and, upon entering, said, "I smell a man!"

The woman, however, said, "That smell certainly comes from your own house."

Then the old woman saw the boots drying over the lamp and asked, "Whose boots are those?"

Ouearnacsuneark replied, "Those are my husband's boots."

The other woman replied, "Those are not your husband's boots. They are round. The soles of these boots are long."

In the evening, the husband of the woman who had hidden the visitor returned. As soon as he entered he said, "I smell a man," and he became very angry; but when Ouearnacsuneark gave him the knife, he calmed down.

Then the visitor came out from his hiding place and the man promised him his assistance. Soon a young man from the other house was heard coming. Ouearnacsuneark's husband gave the visitor a large stone and told him to strike the young man on the head with it because he was actually a wolf. As soon as the wolf passed through the doorway, the man hit him on the head with the stone and killed him.

Immediately the body of the wolf was hauled out of the hut by the wolf's own children. One of the children took some of the flesh and tasted it, saying, "I always thought that father was quite lean, but he is quite delicious."

The visitor rested in the house for a whole day. Then he decided to return home. His host gave him a short stick and told him that whenever he lost his way, he only needed to place the stick in the ground and that whichever way it fell was the way that he had to travel. When he came near his own house, he looked back and saw a cloud of fog rising behind him. Then he knew that the wolves were pursuing him. By running as fast as he could, he reached his home and thus he was saved.

How Inuit Learned the Proper Taboos for when a Bear is Killed

This version is from the Netsilik region.

In the time when there was no difference between humans and animals, their speech was nearly the same. Animals had their own expressions, but otherwise spoke like Inuit, except that their speech was in dialects, as if from a distant and foreign country.

A story is told of a woman who once sought refuge in a bear's dwelling. There she heard bear speech, and from the events she witnessed there she taught people how important it is that the proper taboo is observed when bears are killed. For if a bear's soul is shown the proper respect, the soul will live on and a new bear will be born. It even happens that bears are grateful at having been killed by humans, for the presents that are made to their souls pass to them in the next life.

The Polar Bear and the Boy

This version is from the North Baffin Region.

In the Igloolik area, there was an orphan boy who had no father or mother who stayed with his grandmother. When the men would go hunting by dog team, they would bring the orphan along, but, when returning home with their catch, they would leave him behind.

The orphan would have to walk all the way back to camp. When he finally made it home, night would have long since fallen.

The men of Igloolik would often invite the poor fatherless boy along for the hunt, only to callously leave him behind each time.

So, one day, the men again brought the orphan along to hunt walrus and, again, he was left behind. He was forced to again make the long journey home on foot.

As he was walking, the boy heard footsteps behind him. He turned around to find a large polar bear. As soon as he saw the bear, he harpooned it, and it was then that the realized that it was a shape-shifter.

The shape-shifter said with compassion, "I feel for you when they leave you behind. Let me take care of you for a while."

The polar bear let the orphan ride on his back and started walking toward the water. When they reached the water, the bear dove in and swam toward the island where his fellow polar bears lived. The orphan lived amongst the polar bears while the shape-shifter tried to teach him to be a good hunter.

The orphan had a harpoon and harpoon heads with him. When the boy and the bears went hunting for seals, and the orphan harpooned a seal, a young polar bear would push him aside and steal his kill. Every time they went hunting, the same polar bear did this to him.

So, one day, when returning from hunting, he told the bear who had brought him to the island what was happening. The boy had come to think of the old bear as a grandfather.

"Grandfather," the boy said. "When I catch a seal, this polar bear pushes me and steals it! The same young polar bear does this to me whenever you are not around."

The grandfather replied, "The next time you catch a seal and he starts running towards you, I want you to turn at the last minute and harpoon him."

So, the orphan did what he was told and, when the young polar bear came running towards him, he harpooned it. It then fell to the ground and died. The hunting party then went home, leaving the dead polar bear behind.

During the night, the young polar bear returned to life and came to the camp in search of the boy. It yelled for the boy, "Kanaaqiarjuk come out!"

The grandfather said to the boy, "Don't go out! Don't go out!"

But the young polar bear yelled out again, "Kanaaqiarjuk, come out!"

Again the boy's grandfather said, "Don't go out! Don't go out!"

The polar bear, getting agitated, yelled again, "Kanaaqiarjuk come out!"

The orphan's grandfather finally said, "Ok, you can go out now."

And so he went outside.

The young polar bear that he had harpooned was smiling. It held out Kanaaqiarjuk's harpoon heads and gave them to Kanaaqiarjuk. After that incident, the young polar bear didn't steal any more of Kanaaqiarjuk's catches and never mistreated him again.

When the bears were talking amongst themselves, the young polar bear lay down and said, "I wish that I could push Kanaaqiarjuk and pounce on him while standing on my front legs."

The grandfather bear replied, "You shouldn't wish for things like that, because when our cousins are tormenting us, it is not fun. When dogs surround a polar bear, it is like a frenzy. You have to look out for yourself from every direction."

Now that the orphan was able to hunt and fend for himself, the grandfather sent him on his way home to his family.

The orphan got on the back of the grandfather bear who then jumped in the water and swam to the ice floe. The grandfather swam with the boy on his back until he reached a short walking distance to his home.

And that is the story of how the polar bears helped the orphan to become a skilled hunter, just like a grown man.

The Woman and her Bear Cub

This version is from the South Baffin region.

In a certain village lived an old woman who had adopted a bear cub. In winter, the cub would assist the villagers on the seal hunt by catching seals with its paws, allowing the hunters to easily harpoon them. The cub was very good at catching seals. When it returned from sealing, it would stop in the porch of the hut until its mother brought some blubber to feed it. In time the cub grew up, and the people decided to kill and eat it.

The old woman knew that the people wanted to kill and eat the cub. She warned it, and asked it not to go sealing again. Nevertheless, the cub went off. While sealing, the people tried to kill the cub, but it made its escape and ran home to its mother. It entered the house and sat down on the bed, trembling with fear. Then its mother asked it to escape. At first the cub did not consent, but its foster sister sat on their mother's lap and cried and begged it to run away and save itself. Before the cub ran away, the mother asked it to get some seals for its sister so that she would not starve.

During the summer, the mother went in search of the young bear. When she had been away some time, she hid behind some high rocks, until she saw a bear coming, carrying a seal. The bear came up to her from the shore and put down the seal. Then it went away again. The woman carried the seal to her hut. Another time the mother saw the young bear bringing a ground seal to the shore. She was hiding behind the rocks and the young bear could not see her. The bear put down the seal, took a rest, and went away again. After this it did not return again.

CHAPTER SIX

Animal Fables

The stories in this chapter are all quite short and have a clear message to give. Some of them also include an element of creation, but even in these the purpose is didactic.

The reader may want to be on the lookout for the following:

⊙ *Trickery*
⊙ *False confidence*
⊙ *Correct treatment of children*
⊙ *Consequences of greed*
⊙ *Respect for animals*
⊙ *The power of words*

The Owl and the Lemming

This version is from the South Baffin region.

One day, a lemming was playing about not far from her burrow, when an owl saw her and placed himself right in front of the entrance to her hole.

The owl stood with one foot on each side of the doorway and shouted to the other owls, "Bring two sledges! I have some game that will require two sledges when I have killed it. It cannot go into its house because I have shut the door."

Then the owl sat down in front of the doorway. The lemming was jumping about in front of her den, trying to get in.

Then she said to the owl, "Look up to the sky above you. Spread your legs a little. Spread them out a little more. Bend your head back."

The owl did as he was told, thinking all the time of the great feast he was going to have after he had killed the lemming. Very soon, he stood with one foot on each side of the doorway, his legs bowed out, and his head turned back, looking up to the sky. He did so in order to please the lemming for the few moments she had left to live.

The lemming continued to jump about at a safe distance, but when she saw that the owl's legs were far apart and saw his head bent back, she made a rush for her hole and went in between the owl's spread legs. Then the owl shouted to the others who were coming along with their sledges to turn back home as his game had escaped.

The Owl and the Lemming

This version is from the Kivalliq region.

An owl saw a lemming feeding just outside of his hole.

He flew down and perched at the entrance of the hole and then said to the Lemming,

"Dog teams are coming!"

This frightened the lemming so that he came up close to the hole, pretending that he would rather be eaten by the owl than caught by the dogs.

The lemming said, "I am very fat and you can have a good meal. Take me! If you wish to celebrate before eating me, I will sing while you dance."

The owl agreed and the lemming began to sing while the owl danced. While dancing, the owl looked up to the sky and forgot about the lemming. While he was moving about, he spread his legs far apart, and then the lemming ran between them into his hole. The owl called to him to come out again, saying the dog teams had passed. But the lemming's wife told her husband not to go, but to throw some dirt into the owl's face, which he did.

The Bear and the Caribou

This version is from the South Baffin region.

Once, a bear met a caribou. The bear asked the caribou to arm wrestle to see whose arm was stronger. The caribou consented.

They linked arms and the bear said, "Your forelimb is so much smaller than mine. I am afraid I shall break it."

The caribou retorted, "My leg is strong enough for me to run and jump with."

The bear saw that his arm was ever so much thicker than the caribou's. They began to wrestle, until finally the bear's arm broke. The caribou left the bear in great agony.

The Owl and the Raven

This version is from the South Baffin region.

Two old women, the owl and the raven, were chatting together.

The owl said, "I wish you could make my eyes very sharp."

And the raven said, "I should like to trim your dress."

The owl agreed, and the raven took some soot from her lamp and made the spots which we now see on owl feathers. The owl was very patient until she was told that the decoration of her dress was finished. Then the owl asked permission to decorate the raven's dress. First, she made for her friend a pair of whale-bone boots. The raven agreed to be fitted for the boots, but soon began to hop about. The owl told the raven that she could not do her work well if she did not sit still, but still the raven would not listen. The raven would move from one foot to the other and jump about.

Finally the owl said, "I am going to spill all the oil in my lamp over you if you do not sit still."

Since the raven continued to hop about, the owl became impatient and emptied the lamp oil over her.

Thus the raven became black all over, and flew away, crying, "Qaq, qaq!"

The Foxes

There once was a family of foxes. They were very hungry. The old fox was off sealing.

Late in the evening, he returned and said to his wife, "I tried to find a seal hole and I got on the scent of one. Whenever I ran with my nose down on the ice, I did not notice the scent, but as soon as I raised my head I noticed it. I ran a long way, but still I have not yet found the place."

He asked his wife to make foot protectors for the young foxes, and early the next day they all started out in search of the seal hole the old fox had smelled. When running along the ice, they caught the scent and soon found that it came from a dead whale, which lay on the ground ice. They went right into the whale and lived on its meat. Then they were well supplied. They lived in a house that was all meat.

One day, they saw a number of wolves coming. The foxes were afraid of them. They thought the wolves might want to stay there too, to enjoy the whale meat. In order to drive them away, the old fox devised a ruse.

He jumped on top of the whale and shouted to the wolves, "I smell a whale here, but I cannot see it. There are only rocks here."

The fox had used his magic to make the whale carcass look like rocks.

When they reached the carcass, the wolves saw only rocks, so they departed. When the wolves were gone, the old fox ran back into the whale carcass. He had saved his family from the wolves and they were left in peace to eat the whale.

This version is from the Kivalliq region.

The Fox and the Rabbit

Once upon a time, a fox met a rabbit, and asked him if he had recently caught any seals. The rabbit became angry and said to the fox, "Yes, if you follow my tracks backward, you will find one I have just killed."

The fox went along the rabbit's tracks, but instead of finding a seal, he only found the place where the rabbit had been sleeping in the sun by the side of some rocks. The fox ran away and whenever he met an animal, he would tell him that the rabbit was a great liar.

The Owl and the Two Rabbits

This version is from the Kivalliq region.

An owl saw two rabbits playing close together, and seized them, one in each foot. But they were too strong for him and ran away, pulling the owl behind them.

The owl's wife shouted to him, "Let one of them go, and kill the other!"

But he replied, "The moon will soon disappear and then we shall be hungry. We need both of them."

The rabbits ran on, and when they came to a boulder, one ran to the right side, while the other ran to the left side. The owl was not able to let go quick enough and was torn in two.

The Owl that was Too Greedy

This version is from Northern Greenland (Polar Inuit).

A man out walking came to a cave where the raven, the gull, the hawk, the owl, and the arctic skua all lived together in human shape.

All were anxious to play host to the man, so they went out hunting.

The raven came back with human dung, and on its arrival said to one of its children, "You, with the broad shoulders, fetch the piece of whale skin without blubber from outside: the man must eat."

But the man would not eat it. Only the raven and the gull ate; even the other inhabitants of the cave refused it.

Then the gull went out and came back with many fresh polar cod, which were as delicate as icicles. The man ate of them and thought them good.

Then the hawk went out and caught eider ducks and little auks. The man ate them too, gladly.

The arctic skua, who had no meat, began to vomit and offered the vomit to the man to eat. The man refused it with disgust.

Then at last the owl spoke, saying, "Now let me see if I can provide something for our guest," and he flew off.

On a plain he saw two hares and started to pursue them; but the hares suddenly ran off in different directions, and the owl, trying to go both ways at once, was torn in two. So, he was never able to get food for the man.

This version is from the Kivalliq region.

The Owl and the Bear

Once upon a time, an owl was watching the hole of a lemming, when a bear came near.

The owl said to the bear, "Why are you always walking about?"

The bear replied, "Why are you always standing by the lemming hole?"

The owl asked, angrily, "Why don't you keep yourself clean?"

The bear retorted, "Neither you nor your children can turn your eyes in your head."

The owl said, "Your eyes are green and look like fire."

The bear, advancing towards the owl, said, "Stop where you are, and I'll sit down with you."

The owl, however, was afraid that the bear might kill him, and flew a little ways off. Then the bear pretended to be dead. When the owl saw this, he came nearer and nearer and, when he was very close, the bear caught him in his mouth and killed him.

The Race of the Worm and the Louse

This version is from Northern Greenland (Polar Inuit).

Chapter Six

It is said that our fathers had no lice—lucky people. But once a man lay down to sleep on the ground and the worm and the louse saw him.

The worm, which was a quick mover, said to the louse, "Look! A man! Shall we see which of us can reach him first?"

They started off at a run as quickly as they could, but the worm fell down and the louse arrived first.

"Man does not taste nice at all; the earth is the only food," called out the worm, as it fell down. "I prefer to be the earth's louse."

But the louse found in man both food and home.

And since then men have had lice.

This version is from Northern Greenland (Polar Inuit).

The Raven that was Anxious to be Married

A little sparrow was grieving for her husband, who had not returned. She was fond of him because he used to catch worms for her.

As she sat weeping, a raven came up to her and asked, "What are you crying for?"

"I am crying for my husband, who has not returned. I was fond of him because he caught worms for me," said the sparrow.

"Weeping is not becoming for those who can hop about on the top of the blades of grass. Marry me—me, with my lovely high forehead, broad temples, long beard, and large beak. You shall sleep under my wings and dainty dung shall be your food."

"I will not marry you just because you have a high forehead, broad temples, long beard, and large beak—and because you offer me dung for food."

So, the raven went on his way and went to make love to the wild geese. He was so sick with love that he could not sleep. The wild geese were just about to fly away when he reached them.

"As a silly sparrow has rejected me, I should like to marry you," said the raven to two geese.

"You arrive just as we are about to fly away," said the geese.

"I will come with you," said the raven.

"But see, that is impossible for anyone who cannot rest on the sea. There are no icebergs that way."

"Never mind! I will sail through the air."

And so he took the two geese as his wives.

Then the wild geese set off and the raven went with them; but it was not long before he began to drop behind. He was so tired from having nowhere to rest on such a long journey.

"I need something to rest upon! Place yourselves side by side!" he cried. And his two wives placed themselves side by side on the water, while their comrades went on.

The raven settled himself upon their backs and fell asleep. But when his wives saw the other wild geese getting farther and farther away, they shook the raven off into the sea and flew on.

"Something to rest upon!" shrieked the raven, as it fell with a great splash into the water. It sank to the bottom and drowned. Afterwards, it broke up into small pieces and its soul became little "sea ravens" (black pteropods).

Glossary

Adlet

First Nations people.

Agdlaq

Barren ground grizzly. The barren ground grizzly is a very large, carnivorous brown bear. It lives throughout the Kivalliq region (central Nunavut). Known as akłak in contemporary Inuktitut.

Akla

Barren ground grizzly. See agdlaq.

Amauti

A parka with a special pouch on the back for carrying a child.

Angakkuq (singular) or Angakkuit (plural)

A shaman. An angakok mediates between the human and spirit worlds to heal the sick and to ensure good weather, good hunting, and the community's well-being.

Arctic Skua

The Arctic skua, also known as a parasitic jaeger, is a large, predatory seabird related to gulls. It is brown and has a hooked beak, webbed feet and long pointed wings. It attacks other birds in flight, causing them to disgorge the fish they have caught.

Auk

Auks are a group of short-winged diving seabirds. They have black and white colouring, an upright posture, and a clumsy walk. They fly by flapping their small wings very quickly. They are good swimmers and dive underwater to catch food.

Dancing House

Refers to a very large igloo in which many families can gather for meetings, celebrations, feasting, games, and dancing. Known as a qaggiq in Inuktitut.

Eider Duck

The eider duck is a medium-sized sea duck that breeds in large colonies along arctic coastlines. The male's body is mostly white, with black wings, stomach, and tail. The female is a dull brown colour. Eider ducks have very soft down feathers, which they use to line their nests.

Firestone

A hardened form of quartz that sparks fire when struck against another rock containing the mineral pyrite. Also known as flint.

Hummock

A mound or small hill rising from the land, a marsh, or the sea ice. The soft hummocks of soil and vegetation that rise above the marshy summer tundra make walking easier. Hummocks of ice that rise above the frozen surface of the ocean can make winter travel difficult.

Ijiqat

A shape-shifter that can appear in any form and may be helpful or dangerous. Known as ijiraq in contemporary Inuktitut.

Inuarudligat

A member of the Little People, human-like beings who live out on the land. Known as inugarulligaq in contemporary Inuktitut.

Kamik (singular) or Kamiks (pair)

Boots made of skin. Sealskin is preferred for spring and fall because it is waterproof. Caribou skin is preferred for winter because it is very warm.

Little Auk

The little auk, also known as a dovekie, is a very small member of the auk family (see auk). The little auk has a black head, neck, back, and wings and a white underbelly.

Petrel

Petrels are a large group of web-footed seabirds. They have tubular nostrils over their hooked beak, which they use to feed on fish and algae. Petrels spend most of the year at sea, travelling to land only to breed. The fulmar is the only petrel that migrates to Nunavut. It is grey and white with a yellow beak. The fulmar breeds on cliffs, laying a single egg on the bare rock.

Phalarope

The phalarope is a quick-moving shorebird with long legs and a long, thin beak. Its plumage is soft grey and white with a streak of red at the neck in the summer. When feeding, it swims in a rapid circle, creating a whirlpool that draws food up from the bottom.

Ptarmigan

The ptarmigan is a northern member of the grouse family, related to chickens. It has a plump body and feathered legs and feet. In the winter, the ptarmigan is white. In the summer, its colour changes to brown.

Qajaq

Known as a kayak in English. A long, narrow boat with a watertight covering and a small opening in the top to sit in. Inuit invented the qajaq, originally making the frame from driftwood and the covering from stitched sealskin or other skin.

Qarmaq

A dwelling made with skins stretched over a whalebone frame and covered with thick sod for insulation.

Qulliq

An oil-burning lamp made of soapstone. The soapstone is carved into a crescent-shaped bowl. Seal and whale blubber are used as fuel. Moss, Arctic cotton, and Arctic willow tufts are used as a wick.

Sedna (also known as Nuliajuk)

Known as the mother of all the sea creatures, Sedna has dominion over marine life and life on the land. To ensure good hunting and weather and to prevent sickness, people were to obey many taboos related to Sedna. Only an angakok (shaman; see above) could appease her by travelling to her underwater home.

Snow Bunting

A small, fast-flying bird related to the sparrow. During the breeding season, the male has white plumage with a black back. The female has a gray back. In the winter, the male and female are a mixture of light brown, black, and white. Snow buntings build large nests into rock crevices.

Ulu

A short-handled knife with a curved blade, traditionally used by women in the preparation of food and skins.

References

This publication was composed from archival interviews, present-day interviews, and extensive searches through the works of past ethnographers. Several of these valuable resources are available at libraries and collections around the world.

Here is a list of some of the publications that were used in the research for this book.

Boas, Franz (1888). Central Eskimo. *Bureau of American Ethnology, Annual Report 6*, 399-669.

Boas, Franz (1901). Eskimo of Baffin Land and Hudson Bay. *Bulletin American Museum of Natural History*, 15(1), 1-370.

Boas, Franz (1907). Second Report on the Eskimo of Baffin Land and Hudson Bay. *Bulletin American Museum of Natural History*, 15(2), 371-570

Hawkes, E.W. (1916). The Labrador Eskimo. *Canadian Department of Mines, Geological Survey, Memoir 91, no. 14, Anthropological Series.* Government Printing Bureau: Ottawa.

Jenness, D. (1926). Eskimo Folk-Lore. *Report of the Canadian Arctic Expedition 1913-18*, 13, F.A. Acland: Ottawa.

Kappianaq, G. & Nutaraq, C. (2001). *Inuit Perspectives on the 20th Century: Volume 2 - Travelling and Surviving on Our Land*. Nunavut Arctic College: Iqaluit.

Rasmussen, Knud (1908). *People of the Polar North*. Kegan Paul, Trench, Trubner & Co.: London.

Rasmussen, Knud (1929). *Intellectual Culture of the Iglulik Eskimo*. Gyldendalske Boghandel, Nordisk Forlag: Copenhagen.

Rasmussen, Knud (1930). *Observations on the Intellectual Culture of the Caribou Eskimo*. Gyldendalske Boghandel, Nordisk Forlag: Copenhagen.

Rasmussen, Knud (1931). *The Netsilik Eskimos: Social Life and Spiritual Culture*. Gyldendalske Boghandel, Nordisk Forlag: Copenhagen.

Rink, Hinrich (1875). *Tales and Traditions of the Eskimo*. William Blackwood and Sons: London.